FROM ICE TO FIRE

Recent Titles by Helen Upshall

A HOUSE FULL OF WOMEN
INHERIT THE WIND
LOVE IS MY REASON
THE STRAWBERRY GIRL
TIME-HONOURED VOWS

FROM ICE TO FIRE

Helen Upshall

This title first published in Great Britain 1996 by
SEVERN HOUSE PUBLISHERS LTD of
9–15 High Street, Sutton, Surrey SM1 1DF.
Originally published in 1982 in paperback format only under
the title *Alpine Passion* and pseudonym of *Helen Beaumont*.
This title first published in the USA 1996 by
SEVERN HOUSE PUBLISHERS INC. of
595 Madison Avenue, New York, NY 10022.

Copyright © 1982, 1995 by Helen Upshall.

All rights reserved.
The moral rights of the author have been asserted.

British Library Cataloguing in Publication Data

Upshall, Helen
  From Ice to Fire
  I. Title
  823.914 [F]

  ISBN 0-7278-4911-5

All situations in this publication are fictitious and
any resemblance to living persons is purely coincidental.

Typeset by Palimpsest Book Production Limited,
Polmont, Stirlingshire, Scotland.
Printed and bound in Great Britain by
Hartnolls Ltd, Bodmin, Cornwall.

For my dear friends, the Kiendl family in Deutschlandsberg, Austria, with love and gratitude for happy holidays.

1

Angela went on typing, determined not to glance up yet aware of the big man pacing the floor.

'Three months, I think.' His powerful voice echoed up to the high ceiling and back again.

'Pardon?' she said nervously.

He turned and glared at her. A big man indeed. Powerful muscles evident beneath his coarse army-type shirt, sleeves rolled up above the elbow, baggy breeches narrowing into calf-hugging boots. He had the physique of a military man yet to Angela's knowledge had never been in the Austrian army.

'You will stay no longer than three months, Angela,' he said decisively.

'You mean you won't want me after three months?'

His body relaxed, and his broad face showed amusement. 'I did not mean that, Angela,' he said in a quieter tone. 'By then you will be homesick for England.' He came to stand in front of her desk, leaning heavily on it so that his large, dark brown eyes focused on hers across the typewriter.

Angela felt her cheeks tighten as a faint blush crept into them. In seconds it would spread upwards to her hairline, downwards to her throat. Instinctively she put her hand to the neck of her blouse in an attempt to ward off such embarrassment.

'I've been in Austria for over three months now, Herr Kiegerl,' she began by way of explanation.

He shrugged and splayed his large hands out on her desk. He had a way of raising his eyebrows, bushy black ones to match the thick, curling lashes which fringed his ensnaring dark eyes, and there was a hint of mockery in the wry twist of his sensuous mouth.

Angela readily admitted, though only to herself, that she had qualms about her role as Baron Robert Kiegerl's secretary, and that he intimidated her.

'It's one thing, Angela, to come to our country for a holiday, quite another to remain for ever.'

Now it was Angela's turn to shrug. 'I haven't necessarily planned to stay for ever,' she said. 'But I do feel that something of my heritage is here, so for my mother's sake I'd like to get to know more about the West Steiermark.'

Baron Kiegerl pulled himself up to his full height — about six feet four, Angela guessed. The history of my country is a romantic one — so — Angela — you are a romantic?'

She averted her eyes quickly. 'I . . . I suppose I must be.'

He laughed. 'Delightfully young — just twenty-one — there is time for you to learn our ways, and then you will return to England the wiser for your experiences. But what of your family and friends there? Have you no ties? No young men who will come searching after you?'

She wasn't prepared for the sudden personal inquisition, and her colour deepened. She often thought about Christopher, the boy she'd known from schooldays, whom everyone had thought she would marry. They had been going steady ever since she could remember, but after she had been in Austria for just one month he had written to say he was marrying someone else.

'No ties,' she answered decisively. 'My father is a capable man, my two elder brothers are married. My mother, as you know, is dead.'

'And your father does not mind you prolonging your visit?'

'I think he was a little surprised,' she answered after

some hesitation, 'and perhaps he would agree with you, that in another three months I shall be too homesick to stay.'

'And if you are, Angela, you must say so at once,' he said more gently.

'Thank you,' she said, thinking that she would never let anyone know, however homesick she became.

'When you've finished the letters leave them on my desk,' he requested curtly. 'You must not be late for the meal or my mother will accuse me of working you too hard.'

He strode across the enormous office and went out leaving the solid oak door to slam loudly behind him. The room seemed larger after he had gone.

Angela looked at the mess in her typewriter, tore out the sheet and put a fresh one in. It wouldn't be homesickness which made her leave Baron Robert Kiegerl's employ, it would be a simple case of professional inadequacy.

In spite of her mother being Austrian, her own German was far from fluent. She had sufficient knowledge to be acceptable among her relatives, and it was through her cousins that she had decided to stay in Austria and work. At first the suggestion had been made as a joke, but the idea grew rapidly after she had received the letter from Christopher.

While her mother had been alive the Rainer side of the family had seemed remote — grandparents, aunts, uncles, cousins — people who sent presents at Christmas, wrote occasionally, and visited every six or seven years. But on the sudden death of her mother they suddenly gained new importance.

Her mother's brother, Franz, and his eldest son, Josef, had attended the funeral. Afterwards Angela had made a promise to visit Austria soon.

She had thought of it as a pilgrimage for her mother's sake, but had herself some atavistic love of the country she had never seen. Her father had been a prisoner-of-war in southern Austria, had married a local girl and taken her back to England in 1945.

Still, her mother had settled in England, why could Angela not settle in Austria? She had reasoned with her father who had travelled to see his in-laws with her. He had stayed only three weeks then seemed anxious to return to England. Angela knew how much he missed her mother and considered it strange that he didn't feel the affinity with Deutschlandsberg that she did. After all, he had once promised his wife that when he retired he would take her back to her homeland for as long as she wanted to stay.

Angela knew she was pleasing her grandmother by deciding to live and work in Austria. Grandmother, aunt, uncle and cousins all lived in the old farmhouse high on a hillside overlooking the small town of Deutschlandsberg. It was Josef, her eldest cousin, with whom she got on best. He was thirty-two, kind and warm-hearted yet still unattached. Austrian girls were drawn away from the small towns and villages and lured to big cities like Graz and Vienna.

Most Sundays Josef took Angela out into the surrounding countryside, up into the Little Alps, where some of his cattle were driven for the summer months. They would eat and drink the local wine at a Tyrolean cabin, and join in with the folk who sang and played accordions and guitars.

On one such Sunday Josef had taken her to visit Baron Robert Kiegerl, a wealthy landowner, farmer and fish-breeder.

'You like our town enough to want to stay?' the big farmer had asked in his loud voice. He stretched out his hand and took hers warmly, almost crushing her fingers. She didn't much like the way he had cast his eyes over her. She felt small and weak beside him, and her cotton skirt and tee shirt felt suddenly very flimsy.

Two weeks later she had been invited to return to the baronial hall for an interview with Baron Robert Kiegerl, who needed a secretary. His English was perfect, much better than her German. He had studied in London for two years, he explained.

Angela had been apprehensive both of him and his mother, a small, wiry, distinguished looking seventy-year-old lady. She felt less than confident that she was capable of acting as the Baron's secretary.

Evidently he was doubtful too, she thought now as she tackled the letter for the third time. He said she would be homesick, but she guessed that was his way of suggesting he would only tolerate her for three months at the outside. She couldn't imagine why he'd even considered her for the job when there must be plenty of local girls who needed work of this kind. Angela visualised his ideal secretary as a slightly older and more sophisticated girl, between twenty-five and thirty. The Baron was in his mid-thirties, Josef had told her, though at times he looked even older, especially when he was wearing his thick, dark-rimmed reading glasses. Angela liked him better then — without his glasses his bold stare knocked her off balance, making her feel vulnerable and exposed.

She was doubtful about what she had let herself in for. It hadn't occurred to her that she would be expected to live in, but that had been a condition of employment.

'From Monday to Friday I shall need you on hand from dawn to dusk,' he had told her, adding with a teasing glint, 'we work our staff like slaves. At weekends you can visit your uncle's farm or you can keep my mother company. You'll be good for her, and she'll teach you to speak much better German.'

He was outspoken, but so were her Austrian relatives. At first she had found it unnerving, but now that she was getting used to it, found that it was an attractive quality.

Angela managed to get the letter finished without any more mistakes. She wished she had an office to herself where she could work undisturbed. It wasn't that the Baron was in the office that much, but he invariably brought visitors, staff, or business colleagues there, and they always talked noisily over a glass of wine.

But even without visitors, wherever the big man went he made his presence felt. It was his domain. He was the key figure, the dominant owner of a vast estate which included stables and some two dozen horses, a farm with cattle and chickens, a picturesque lake set among woodland, fields of maize cob and other crops, and the fish farm — all of which needed numerous workers.

She fitted the cover over the modern electric typewriter, put the letters on her boss's desk, switched off the lights and went through a passageway of stone floors and arches to the main part of the house.

A huge oak door with heavy iron hinges opened at a twist of the ringed handle and she was in a square hall where curved wooden stairs ascended on two sides to the gallery and floor above. As yet Angela was still none too sure of her way around. Her bedroom was on the first floor just at the top of the left-hand staircase. Paintings, shields, guns and antlers decorated the walls, giving the hall and passageways a feudal air, but the moment she stepped into her room she was among 20th century luxuries.

One thing she admired above all else in Austria was the natural wood from which beds, cupboards, fitments, tables and chairs were all expertly made. It made the room seem warmer. The polished parquet flooring was covered wtih colourful rugs chiefly in green and beige, and the bedspreads and curtains were of cheerful floral material. Everything she could want had been provided. Not only did she have her own bathroom, but it included a shower, and there was always plenty of hot water.

Angela looked at her watch. It was almost seven o'clock and Frau Kiegerl had told her that the evening meal would be at seven-thirty. She quickly showered and dressed in an emerald-green dress which heightened the shade of her green eyes and offset her rick dark hair.

As she closed the door behind her, feeling somewhat timid at the prospect of a fairly formal dinner, a door on the opposite side of the landing opened and the Baron himself appeared. He looked quite different now in a smart, well-cut suit of dark blue with a grey thread woven into it. He didn't seem quite so bulky as when he was dressed for farm-work, but as he came up to stand beside Angela she was aware of his massive physique.

'Angela!' He had a delightful way of pronouncing her name, emphasising the last syllable. She knew he enjoyed rolling it off his tongue. 'We are one minute late,' he said, glancing at his watch, and with his hand firmly round her shoulder he guided her to the stairs. His awesome masculine strength made her tingle with apprehension. He was not a man anyone would cross lightly, she thought. Was this the reason he had not married? Perhaps he could not find a woman of a strength to match his own. Usually there was an earthly smell about him, leathery, animal, sometimes even fishy, but now as he hurried her along the landing to the farthest staircase she caught a whiff of male freshness, the merest hint of cologne.

'I tell my mother that we should organise a one-way system on these stairs — up that end, down this way,' he said jovially as they began to descend the wide, carpeted treads. He laughed heartily, and she felt his muscles against her side. She would have moved away, but he made no attempt to let her go until they had reached the dining room, where his mother stood with another woman.

Angela felt her heart miss a beat. The woman was *so* beautiful!

'Lilli!' the Baron exclaimed. 'A surprise!' He took her arms gently in his strong hands and kissed her forcefully. 'Let me introduce you to my English secretary — Fräulein Angela de Vere.'

The older woman — she could be in her late twenties or thirties, Angela couldn't judge — smiled warmly and shook Angela's hand.

'Frau Gosch,' Robert introduced her.

'Please call me Lilli.'

Angela smiled shyly.

'I think you will find it easier to call me Robert, Angela,' the big man said, going to the sideboard and selecting a drink.

The woman went to his side and said something softly at which they both laughed. Angela guessed that it was a joke at her expense and felt disconcerted.

Robert's mother, noticing Angela's discomfort, spoke sharply. Immediately Robert turned and handed Angela a glass of white wine.

'Forgive us, Angela, my dear,' he apologised. 'Lilli is mocking me as sisters do.'

'Because you are young and pretty, Angela,' Lilli explained, going to her and placing a hand on her arm. 'Perhaps you can make him a nicer man to work for. I think it is only fair that you should know no woman in her right senses would ever work for the great Robert.' She laughed up at her brother, her dark eyes (so much like his) sparkling mischievously.

'Be quiet, woman,' Robert retorted. 'Let Angela find out for herself what a brute I am.' He looked down at Angela, his expression one of amusement at her puzzled frown. 'It's not true, Angela,' he assured her. 'Take no notice of these women.' He turned towards them. 'Can't you see the alarm in Angela's face?'

'She will find out for herself,' Frau Kiegerl said firmly. 'And if he is any trouble, Angela, you will come and tell me at once, will you not?'

Angela laughed. 'I shall be pleased to have someone on my side by the sound of things.'

'But mothers are always on the side of their sons. Is that not so, Mama?' Robert demanded.

Frau Kiegerl grunted disdainfully and, lifting her ebony stick, gave her son a tap on his backside.

'There's not so much harm in you. Your size may frighten some, but I know that you can be gentle when it suits you.'

Robert went to the side of the table and started to carve from a huge joint of beef. Frau Kiegerl took her place at the head of the table, indicating that Angela should sit on her left hand side as she usually did. Robert's place was at his mother's right immediately opposite Angela. So far during the few days she had been at the hall there had only been the three of them, often just Frau Kiegerl and Angela, so that she had become used to the food and custom at the table.

As the meal progressed Lilli told Angela that she too had been partly educated in England, and wanted to know how much had changed there.

'You are a brave girl,' Lilli said, 'to create such an upheaval in your life. Will you not be homesick?'

Robert was quick to answer for her. 'Of course she will be, just as you were at twenty-one years old,' he reminded her.

'I'm determined not to think about it,' Angela said, with more spirit than she actually felt.

Robert laughed. 'I think she will be soon longing for the young Englishmen.'

'Angela comes from a good family,' Frau Kiegerl interrupted. 'Her grandmother and I went to school together.'

'Josef and I also were at agricultural college together,' Robert said.

'Married to the land, you see, Anglea,' Lilli said. 'It's a

shame that modern girls all flock to the large towns.'

'You sound eager to marry me off, *meine lieb*,' Robert said to his sister. 'I suppose you see me as an old man dependent upon his elder sister?'

Angela looked up quickly, hardly able to believe that Lilli was older than Robert.

Robert noticed her surprise. 'You think Lilli is younger than I?' he acknowledged with a smug grin.

'I . . . I hadn't really thought — ' Angela began awkwardly.

'She is beautiful,' he complimented, then added mischievously, 'for a middle-aged lady!'

Lilli, who was sitting next to her brother, gave him a dig. 'There is not so much difference between us, remember,' she admonished with a laugh.

Angela was amused at the light-hearted banter, which made her feel more at home. She remembered the fun she had shared with her brothers in the past — all so long ago now.

After dinner, back in her own room, she sat down with pen and paper to write to her father. For a time she simply stared at the flowers on the curtains, unable to make a start. She longed to enquire after Christopher. She couldn't quite rid herself of the affection she still felt for him, however badly he had treated her.

But it was only in quiet moments like this that she felt any real regret over the break between them. Now that they were separated, she realised that there had not been the bond between them which was necessary for marriage.

If he had really loved her he would have understood the dreadful shock her mother's death had been, both physically and emotionally. He would have made allowances for her lack of response to his lovemaking, instead of which he had accused her of being frigid.

'Never more than lukewarm,' he'd condemned her in his frustration, 'and now like an iceberg. Austria will be the best place for you, Angie. Perhaps up on those snow-clad mountains tops you'll freeze and be glad to find someone to thaw you out.'

She'd been so hurt at his cruel spite, but in her heart she knew that he had assessed the situation correctly. She wasn't frigid, she tried to console herself, of course she wasn't. There had been many moments of passion even though the persuasion came from Christopher. He had frightened her a little, always wanting, taking, demanding, and she had not been ready to give. This must have meant she wasn't truly in love with him, as she had supposed. Her heart didn't ache with longing for him; in fact, as the weeks had passed she thought less and less of him. The news of his love for someone else had come as a shock, but she had also felt a touch of relief. The time had come to do something different.

So she had come to Deutschlandsberg, to her mother's family.

The Kiegerl estate was some twelve miles from the town. The local village was inhabited entirely by people who worked for Baron Kiegerl. Her friends back home would be impressed by the place, although for the present perhaps it was best to keep it to herself.

It seemed too good to be true — the job which she felt sure she would enjoy given time (vastly different from her past employment as secretary to a property developer) and the chance to live on a great estate in a large house.

From the outside, the house was no enchanted castle, not even a distinguished manor house, just a very solid old building with heavy doors and lots of windows. It was the people inside the house that were impressive, Angela decided, twirling her pen between her fingers, but she wasn't sure how best to describe them to her father. He had written that he was surprised she had found work in such a rural area, and seemed to think it might consist of milking cows.

This was Angela's first taste of being entirely independent, but gnawing away at the back of her mind was the guilty feeling that her proper place was at home, caring for her bereaved father. Guilt now was coupled with cowardice: she couldn't imagine how she would face her friends since Christopher had married someone else.

Her light burned late and, when she went down for breakfast next morning, she was heavy-eyed.

Robert came in just as Angela sat down. *'Guten morgen,'* he said in his masterly tone. She knew that already he had been at work for two or three hours. 'You did not sleep well, Angela?'

'Yes — very well,' she assured him, looking puzzled.

'But your light was on until very late. Was something troubling you?'

'No, I was writing to my father.'

'And was that such a difficult task?'

She shook her head. 'Of course not,' she answered. 'There was a lot to tell him.'

The flicker of a smile played round Robert's mouth as he poured coffee. Eva, the cook-housekeeper, brought his bacon and eggs, and he ordered the same for Angela.

'Oh no,' she said, 'I'm late, I should be in the office.'

Robert Kiegerl leaned back and spoke to Eva again and she hurried away laughing, only to return in a very few minutes with some rather frizzled-up rashers and fried eggs.

'You shouldn't have,' Angela complained. 'I don't eat a cooked breakfast.'

'All English people eat a large breakfast,' Robert insisted.

'Not these days, and not when I'm working,' she argued.

'That is when you need it most, Angela, when you are working,' he said adamantly, then seeing her looking at her plate without much relish he added with a laugh, 'The

English are best at cooking breakfast, though not at cooking anything else, or so people say!'

'When Eva has a day off I'll do it for you,' Angela said.

Robert looked at her, pushing his glasses up on his nose as if to see more clearly. 'Eva never takes a day off. She wouldn't know how to use it if she had one. Besides, where could she go? Her life is here — a servant but also one of the family. She is irreplaceable, Angela. But one day you shall cook my breakfast for me.'

It was the suggestive tone of his voice which sent the blood coursing through her veins too rapidly for such an early hour, colouring her cheeks with a pink glow. She had felt more comfortable in his presence this morning, without his mother's shrewd glances and with his own observant eyes shaded by spectacles. But he was still the same man, dominant, powerful: a man who unnerved her yet at the same time disturbed some deep emotion she was unable to identify.

She felt his keen eyes watching her as she started to eat.

'I see you understand the implication,' he continued. 'Yes, Angela, a man has certain rights over his secretary. Englishmen are renowned for leaving their wives to live with their secretaries,' he shrugged, 'or to marry them. It is — I think you would say — a foregone conclusion that most men's secretaries become their mistresses?'

'No, I most certainly would not say,' she said hotly.

He threw back his head and laughed at her. He had a booming laugh to match his size, yet his amusement had the effect of putting Angela at ease. She assumed that he was only teasing her.

All the same it made her wonder what kind of a man he was. At first she had suspected he was concerned only with money and business, but as the days passed she recognised signs of a good boss, one who cared about the people who worked for him as well as the livestock he reared and the land he loved.

But what were his relationships with women? Was he one of those men for whom no other woman could possibly match his mother? Where did he look for sexual stimulation or satisfaction? Did he really expect his secretary to fulfil this need as well?

Lilli had joked about his past secretaries and how badly he treated them. Perhaps his sister was unaware of the demands he made on them. Perhaps that was why the distinguished Baron Robert Kiegerl knew that Angela could only last for three months.

She would need to be on her guard. She must never ever trust him. Now, after what he had said, she would be terrified of being alone with him — what strength had she to fight off such a powerful man?

But such thoughts faded as the day's work took up all her attention. Each day she learned a little more, became more proficient in her use of the language.

Some days were disappointing though, days when she seemed unable to do anything right. On one such day, Robert had been working in the office, frequently interrupted by the telephone, visiting salesmen, and staff problems. She sighed as she struggled to understand her notes for a report she was typing.

A man a few years younger than Robert had called to see him and they talked and laughed loudly. Angela had caught the gist of their conversation about Robert's horses, but now Robert was leaning with his back against a filing cabinet, his arms folded across his waist and his eyes on Angela. She guessed that he would see she was having trouble. The other man too was looking at her, and as they continued to talk loudly Angela found it impossible to concentrate.

At last a feeling of despair she glanced up at the two men.

'Yes, Angela,' Robert said with a sympathetic smile, 'We would like some coffee before Andreas returns to Graz.'

She got up thankfully and went out to the small kitchen. While the two men were drinking their coffee Angela returned to the kitchen. It was getting late. She knew that Robert wanted the report this evening so she would offer to return after dinner to complete it. So far he hadn't complained too much about her work. She was mindful of the fact that he was making allowances for her inefficiencies but most of these arose when he was also working in the office. She wouldn't admit that his very presence was a distraction, but she felt that she would concentrate better if she was able to work alone. There were plenty of rooms, all she needed was a place to herself.

She heard the men's voices drawing closer. To her surprise they came into the kitchen.

'Andreas is leaving, Angela,' Robert informed her as if it concerned her personally.

The younger man came forward, his hand outstretched. 'It's been a pleasure to meet you, Angela,' he said, clasping her hand warmly. 'I've just been telling Robert what a lucky fellow he is. We shall meet again soon, I hope.'

He spoke English with a strong accent, unlike Robert who could almost have passed for English. No doubt Andreas had not been able to study in England. His smile was genuine, and his pale blue eyes conveyed his interest.

After he had gone Angela returned to her desk. Robert came to stand by her side. 'Time you finished, Angela,' he said kindly.

'Robert,' she said, gazing up at him, hoping that her friendly approach would gain his consideration. 'I'm making a hash of this. I . . . I get on better when I'm working alone. Is it — would it be possible for me to have a room of my own to work in?'

2

By his momentary silence she realised her request had surprised him.

'An unusual request,' he said thoughtfully. 'None of my previous secretaries have been uncomfortable here.'

'But I can't be compared with them,' she said hurriedly. 'I mean, I know I can't hope to be as competent as they.'

'Have I complained?' he asked softly.

'No — but you've had cause to on occasion. I do know my own limits.'

'As a secretary — or as a woman, Angela?' His head came down closer to hers.

She felt a tight knot in her stomach. They were alone, it was dark outside, and suddenly she was afraid of him.

'I just feel I'd be able to concentrate better on my own,' she said in a trembling voice, ignoring the second half of his question.

He took her hand, his other round her shoulder. With compelling force he drew her to her feet.

'Whatever would people think if I shut you away on your own, *meine lieb?*' She knew what was going to happen . . . 'No, Angela, you may not have an office to yourself — I need you, here with me.'

His arms encased her slim body and she felt his knees bend so that he could reach down to match his sensuous lips to hers. She expected to feel his body hard against hers but it was flexible, warm and intimate as he persuaded her lips to part in unison with his.

She hadn't expected him to prove his need of a woman so quickly. As she felt his throbbing pulse urgently responding to her feminine attractions she struggled to push him away.

'No, Robert,' she managed to say even as his lips toyed with hers. 'I didn't come to work for you for this.'

'Stop struggling, Angela — a little love-making is a comfort. You are very desirable — you were to Andreas, so I think I must stake my claim before — '

'You don't have a claim on me,' she told him angrily. 'Let me go, I haven't finished the report yet.'

'We'll do it together after dinner.'

'No,' she cried adamantly. 'I want to work alone.'

He still held her fast. 'You mean I disturb you so much?'

'There are too many distractions,' she protested vehemently. 'The language — I need to be able to concentrate.'

He cradled her stiffened body in his arms. 'You women,' he growled, 'you make too much of your show of protest. Your resistance does not fool me, *meine lieb*. I will make you surrender.' His mouth was smooth and challenging, and in spite of her rebellious anger she found herself kissing him back, her whole body stimulated by his powerful masculinity.

'This isn't right, Robert. I came here only as your secretary. I want to work for you, and I want to do it well.'

'As I said I have no complaints — yet. Only that you almost convince me that you don't expect me to make love to you. I've had secretaries before, Angela. The tight skirt, the sweater, he indicated her outline with his hands, 'your top buttons undone on your blouse, isn't this meant to be an invitation?'

'Certainly not! I never thought of such a thing,' she cried, outraged.

He held her quivering chin between his fingers and

searched her green eyes with curiosity.

'Your reaction tells me differently . . . Perhaps you are too unsure of yourself as yet,' he said, still studying her critically.

'Please don't judge me by the other women who have been your secretaries. I did not take the job you offered me expecting to be kissed, pawed — or made love to.'

He had relaxed his hold briefly, but now he pulled her savagely to him kissing her violently.

'I'll dictate the terms of our contract,' he said between his teeth, forcefully crushing her body beneath his great hands until she thought she was going to be pounded to pulp. 'You'll fulfil your obligations without question whether it's working out the milk yield, paying the workers' wages, typing letters or satisfying me in bed!'

'You're a maniac,' she yelled at him. 'A savage beast and you can have my notice now this minute.'

He stood back and grinned. 'Go on then,' he mocked. 'Out into the night — find your own way back to your uncle's farm — tell them what a brute I am, but don't forget to tell them that you are as cold as the snow up on the mountains.'

From somewhere a long way off the sound of a gong could be heard.

'Dinner,' he announced with a grin, 'so now you can run to Mama and tell her what a wicked son she has.'

'I suspect she already knows,' she hissed at him, knowing full well that she wouldn't tell a single soul what had taken place during the last hour, least of all his mother.

She ran from him, hating him with a new fury for the way he manipulated her. She put her head round the dining-room door.

'Frau Kiegerl — I'm so sorry,' she apologised, 'I'm afraid I'm not dressed for dinner.'

.Robert came up behind her, his large hands spanning

her waist as he pushed her inside the room. 'Neither am I, Mama, but we still have work to do.'

'You must not work Angela so hard,' his mother scolded.

'It is not all work, Mama. We take time off to play a little also — isn't that right, Angela?'

Angela ignored him. 'Could I just go and freshen up?' she asked.

'Five minutes, my dear,' Frau Kiegerl said, and Angela sped upstairs with Robert chasing after her.

He caught up with her at the door, placed his hand over hers on the door handle and went with her inside, unzipping her skirt, unbuttoning her blouse, teasing until she was hot and flustered. He picked her up and tossed her on to the bed as it were a trampoline.

'Mama said five minutes,' he said wickedly. 'Will it take that long, Angela? Will you dare me to arouse some passion in you — take you to the point of no return in just five minutes?'

Angela quickly rolled off the bed on the other side.

'Get out,' she snapped.

He laughed. 'Speed is not the essence of pleasure, Angela! No, when you surrender to me it will be a long night of loving.' He went out, slamming the door.

She was thankful to be able to splash cold water on her face and tidy her hair so that she felt clean of that monster's mauling hands. Never had she anticipated that he was going to turn into such a fiend. He knew, the swine, that she'd never tell anyone about his behaviour. No matter how much she hated him he was in the happy position of being thought of as honourable, and above reproach in every respect.

Piping hot soup was already on the table in the dining room and while they ate Frau Kiegerl and Robert conversed about estate matters.

Robert hardly seemed to notice Angela. His sleeves

were rolled up and she was acutely aware of the thick black hair which covered his arms. His skin was a dark tan, his fingers elegantly long, not like those of a hardworking farmer. Why was she so aware of him? she wondered. She had been from their first meeting. Now, those same hands had done all manner of things to her body, awakening senses which she was determined to keep locked away.

'Are you going to your relatives for the weekend?'

She looked up quickly, 'Yes. Josef will come for me about twelve, but I'll finish that report tonight if that's what's bothering you,' she said.

'Not tonight, Angela. I'll get you up at six in the morning.'

Frau Kiegerl made a guttural sound of rebuke, but when Angela dared to glance at Robert he smiled gently to her, disssolving the anger she felt.

'I can get up at six,' she said haughtily. 'I did every day when I first arrived in Deutschlandsberg.'

'You were not ready to get up at six the other morning,' he reminded her.

'I will do the report though,' she promised. 'Tonight if you like.' She sent him a warning glance, insinuating that she would expect to have the office to herself.

'Not tonight, Angela,' he repeated. 'I have more work to do — we might disturb each other.'

There was a wealth of meaning in his voice which she chose to ignore.

'Is it so important?' Frau Kiegerl questioned.

'Yes,' he answered. 'A report for the tax inspector who is coming at the weekend.'

His mother grunted. 'What is he doing working at the weekend?' she asked with impatience.

Robert sighed. 'He came a week ago and it was not ready, Mama. I suggested he might like to come tomorrow so that he could ride a little, perhaps shoot, fish for our best trout in the lake.'

'A-ha!' Frau Kiergerl said accusingly, 'so you try to keep in with this tax inspector?'

'He happens to be a friend of mine,' Robert said. 'Now, if you'll excuse me I must get back to the office. I'll say goodnight to you both.' He stooped to kiss his mother on her cheek and at the door paused. Angela turned to see why he was still there. By his expression and the quick lifting of one eyebrow she realised that she had not wished him goodnight, so she did so in a low conciliatory voice. She hoped his mother had not noticed the hesitation before he left the room or the colour flooding her cheeks.

'Let us take our coffee into the sitting room, Angela my dear. It is more cosy there — and Eva can clear away here.'

Angela carried the tray across the hall into a smaller room. It was a pleasant sitting room where, Frau Kiegerl explained, she and Robert liked to sit in the winter evenings to watch television or read.

'Not that Robert is here much to keep me company,' she said with a note of disappointment. 'I suppose I should be grateful that he is still a bachelor. One day he will have a wife, and then I must sit here alone. She will want him to herself, and they will make some rooms into a modern apartment for themselves.' She smiled wistfully at Angela. 'You will be thinking that I am a selfish old woman.'

'No, of course not,' Angela hastened to assure her. 'But you would like him to marry I expect?'

Frau Kiegerl sipped her coffee. 'To the right girl,' she conceded. 'Someone who will take an interest in the estate and help him to keep it going. Taxes are heavy, expenses are very great, and I worry that Robert has to work so hard to keep it all in good order, and to keep me too. It will be better for him when I am gone.'

'I'm sure Robert wouldn't like to hear you talk like that, Frau Kiegerl. You're not old and there are lots of things you do to help him. This house, for instance, if you were not here he would be dependent on Eva to run things.'

'Ah — my dear, that is what concerns me. Robert is a lively man who is fond of women. I know my son, and he finds certain women very attractive. If anything happened to me, my dear, I am afraid he would marry one of these town girls, the first one available. They chase him, you know, they telephone him at night and they write to him and even come to visit — then I make myself seen, you understand, and they don't come again. They would not fit in at the hall. Robert's wife must be a girl of simple tastes and one who is not afraid of hard work. She will have to love him greatly, I think, to put up with the kind of life Robert enjoys. His work is his life. All the same he is warm-hearted and would be good to the right girl. But that is enough. Tell me, Angela, all about England. I went there, you know, in the thirties.'

* * *

Next morning Angela's travelling alarm clock rang at six-thirty. She stretched lazily, then remembering she had the report to finish got up and dressed, putting on jeans and sweater as she guessed the office might be chilly at this hour. She drew back her curtains and lifted a slat of the venetian blind. It was drizzling with rain and she could see angry black clouds thickening up, blotting out the mountain top. It looked as if she would have to be content with a quiet weekend at her uncle's farm, instead of going out into the countryside or even into Graz, but it was fun to be with her mother's family, and she knew that her grandmother would be anxious to see her.

Angela crept downstairs quietly. To her surprise the aroma of coffee filled the corridor before she reached the office. She found it percolating noisily with cups and saucers set out on a tray nearby.

Robert was not in the office. She supposed the coffee must be waiting for him. The delicious smell was making her thirsty, but the urge to complete the report for Robert kept her steadily working. She was progressing well and at eight o'clock took the final sheet out of the typewriter. Now she had to check it all. As she stretched, yawning, she heard the unmistakable sound of a door closing, then the heavy tread of Robert's boots.

'You've had coffee?' he asked abruptly, appearing in the doorway.

She looked up. 'I thought it was for you and whoever you're expecting,' she said.

'It was for you, Angela,' he replied, then turned and went out again. He came back carrying two cups of coffee which he put down on his desk.

'How's it going?' he asked.

'I've finished, apart from checking it over.'

'Good. We'll have coffee first, and then you can read it while I check your copy.'

'I'm sure I can manage. You must have other things to do.'

'For today, Angela, this report is top priority, and I want you to be ready when Josef comes for you.'

'That's hours away.'

'Time passes quickly — though it looks as if it's going to be a dreary weekend.'

But Robert was wrong. By midday, the clouds had cleared away. Angela drove off with Josef in bright sunshine.

Her grandmother and all the family were eager to know how she had got on working at the hall. Angela explained about the work and the pleasant room she had been given as her own, but she was careful not to voice her opinion of the Baron.

On Sunday afternoon Josef drove her to another village some miles away to see the farmer to whom he would sell the grapes from the vineyard when the October harvest had been gathered in.

'In the old days,' he explained, 'as I'm sure your mother has told you, everyone helped to pick the grapes. It was a time of festival in the autumn when the weather is good and the harvest of grapes just ready. Then the wine was made, and we all hoped for a good yield and the best vintage wine. Now, labour costs are too high, so the grapes are gathered and sold to this elderly farmer who still makes the Schilcher wine, the speciality of the Steiermark.'

'It must have been great fun in the old days. I can just imagine the women with brightly-coloured scarves over their hair all dressed in cotton dresses and aprons, singing folk songs as they worked in the vineyard,' Angela enthused.

'*Wein-garten*,' Josef corrected with a smile.

'Wine-garden — it sounds so much more romantic than vineyard,' she said.

'There's nowhere in the world more romantic than our country, Angela,' Josef said with pride.

The weekend passed all too quickly. Josef was good company, always kind and attentive, and it was late evening when he pulled up in the courtyard of the hall again.

Almost at once a light spilled out on to the gravel path as the door opened and Robert stood silhouetted in the darkness.

'Ah — Robert is making sure I return you to him safely,' Josef said and he got out of the car, hurrying round to help Angela out.

The two men shook hands, and Robert then took Angela's in his large one.

'You've had an enjoyable time, Angela?' he asked.

'Mm — very nice,' she replied happily.

'Josef — next weekend we're having a party, so we

should like Angela to spend the weekend with us here, to help Mama a little perhaps.'

Angela stiffened with annoyance. He was taking her for granted. Why wasn't he asking her instead of telling Josef?

'There will be a barbecue on Saturday and various sporting activities on Sunday until about four o'clock,' he went on. 'You will be most welcome to come and join us if you can spare the time. I know Angela would like you to.'

He pinched her cheek rather brutally. Josef seemed enthusiastic and promised that he would telephone later in the week to confirm the arrangements. Then he put his arm around Angela's waist and kissed her warmly as he said goodbye.

Robert pointedly walked back inside leaving her and Josef together.

'Josef, are you sure you want to come here next weekend?' she asked softly. He kissed her again, holding her close.

'Yes, Angela, it sounds as if it will be a good time. Why? Do you think I shouldn't come because you work here?'

'No — no, it's not that — I think he's got a cheek,' she whispered. 'He could have asked *me* if I minded working over the weekend.'

Josef laughed. 'Not Robert Kiegerl — he owns the people who work for him. But you'll enjoy it, his parties are renowned.'

Angela groaned. 'How often is this likely to occur?'

'Not every week,' Josef laughed. 'I suppose three or four times a year. Robert will make it up to you — he's extremely good to his staff.'

'As long as they're obedient,' she murmured testily.

'Here in the country, Angela, we're still a little old-fashioned. On large estates like this one the owner expects loyalty, that is all.'

'I hope Grandma won't mind.'

'I'll explain. She'll be more concerned that you're

pleasing the Baron. Go now, he is waiting to lock up.'

Angela ran to the doorway and turned to wave to her cousin as he turned in the courtyard, and drove off along the narrow lane. Robert was still standing by the door.

'I hope I haven't kept you up?' Angela said as she watched Robert close the heavy door decisively, turning the enormous iron key and reaching up to slide the heavy bolts across.

'I seldom go to bed before midnight, Angela. Unlike you I need only a few hours sleep.'

She went through to the hall and began to ascend the stairs.

'You could have brought Josef inside.'

'It's late,' she answered, 'and I've been at the farm all weekend.' Robert seemed to fill the hall, not so much by his size as by the bristling displeasure which showed in his expression. He hadn't liked the way Josef had kissed her.

'Goodnight, Robert,' she whispered.

Inside her room she looked doubtingly at the door. It was closed very firmly and had a noisy handle, but there was no lock or bolt. She listened, but the house was still. Robert had said that he didn't go to bed until midnight. It was nearly that now, but she was too tired to keep alert any longer so she went to bed and tried to imagine what work the forthcoming party would involve.

When Angela opened the post next morning she soon learned the names of the expected guests. Replies from invitations sent out before her employment commenced arrived during the next three days.

'So what is the final total, Angela?' Robert asked mid-week when he came into the office after breakfast.

'Unlucky number,' she said. 'Thirteen.'

'Without the family,' Robert reminded her with a smile.

'Fifteen then,' she corrected.

'Sixteen, Angela, counting yourself.'

'I'm not family,' she replied, giving him a sly glance.

'All right then,' he admonished sharply and in his usual loud voice. 'You are a guest — I will write you an invitation and expect to receive a reply — or,' he said, coming to lean in his favourite place in front of her desk so that he could look closely into her face, 'will you accept a verbal invitation?'

Angela hesitated. She had lost much of her nervousness now in his presence. She had come to understand him better and knew that he liked nothing better than to tease, so, in a familiar way she answered: 'Yes, thank you, Baron Kiegerl. I am pleased to accept even though it is such short notice.'

He was not wearing his spectacles and as Angela searched his eyes for a hint of mischief, she saw none there. They stared at one another across the typewriter. At length he pulled himself up and said: 'I did not realise how much Josef mattered to you.'

'All my family matter to me,' she said. 'That's the reason I chose to stay here and work.'

'If you say so, Angela.' He was doing his usual circular pacing before he returned to her desk. 'There is more to it than that, I think! Perhaps you are a coward — oh, not in the face of danger I'm sure — but the young Englishman would not wait while you satisfied your curiosity concerning your family, and now you cannot go home and face him when he has married someone else. Is that not right, Angela?'

'I don't really think it's any of your business,' she said, her cheeks flaming angrily.

'It will be my business if you should suddenly want to rush back to England, or indeed if you should think to marry Josef.'

'Marry Josef!' she echoed, amazed. 'We're cousins!'

'So? That is no great problem is it?'

'It wouldn't be if we loved each other in that way.'

'Ah — Angela!' He waved a finger at her. 'There is only

one way to love — and you have much to learn about the subject of love, I think.'

'Well I don't wish to learn from you,' she answered shortly.

This surprisingly amused him and he laughed heartily, and then returning to her side he placed his hand on the nape of her neck, gripping it fiercely.

'While you are in my employ you will learn much, Angela,' he said, against her ear. 'Now — back to work. You will draw up a list of guests, and then you will work with Mama today, who will tell you which rooms our guests will occupy. There will be menus to prepare and a schedule of events to type for each guest. I think you will find it interesting — you shall be my courier — my aide de camp.'

Angela again felt that she was being used. What good would she be as a courier when she had no idea what events were to take place at this party, but Frau Kiegerl soon put her mind at rest.

'Robert feels I need help on these occasions, my dear,' she said, tucking her arm through Angela's and leading her up the staircase and through the corridor which led to the west side of the house. 'He is so fond of company and would have liked to run regular house parties for paying guests. They do it in the tourist areas, but here there is not so much for the tourist to see, only those who like the country and farm life.'

'I'm sure it would be a great attraction,' Angela said. 'It would have to be publicised, and run on a commerical basis.'

'Robert seriously considered it some years ago — but he needs a wife to work with him, so he chose to become a fish farmer as another means of increasing our revenue.'

They had reached the end of the long carpeted passage and Frau Kiegerl unlocked an arched door. Angela couldn't help but gasp at the airy lightness of this wing.

They went from room to room, all splendidly decorated with pastel-coloured walls and matching venetian blinds. Frau Kiegerl drew back the heavy brocade curtains and opened the venetian blinds in each room to let in the late summer sunshine. Bed coverings matched the curtains, and even the oriental rugs which partially covered the parquet flooring blended in with the colour schemes.

She didn't count the rooms, but she felt certain there were sufficient to house twice as many guests as were on the list.

Frau Kiegerl sat down in an easy chair in one of the rooms. 'Now, Angela, my dear, how many doubles do we need?'

'Herr and Frau Rudolph Gosch,' Angela read from the paper in her hand.

'Ah — that's Lilli and her husband. They have a room of their own similar to yours, next to mine,' she explained.

So Lilli had a husband, Angela observed. She went on reading down the page, discovering that there were three other married couples, which meant that five single rooms were required.

'The single guests must be put in twin-bedded rooms,' Frau Kiegerl explained. 'Let me see, dear Dr Weiss is coming. Robert invites him to keep me company. A very dear friend of my late husband's — a notary of great repute, and I'm very fond of him, but if my children think I'm going to be persuaded to marry again they are mistaken. Not until Robert finds a wife.'

Angela laughed. 'And perhaps Robert is saying that he will not marry until his Mama has found a husband.'

Frau Kiegerl shook her head and smiled wistfully. 'Not my Robert. If and when he meets the genuine girl he will sweep her off her feet, and she and I will have to tolerate each other. But that, Angela, is what I want, for Robert to be happy and he is not. He puts on this air of — how d'you say in England? — devil-may-care? Yes, so that no one knows what he really feels. He tries to hide it from me, but I know.'

Angela hesitated before asking: 'Has he been let down? Has he been hurt in the past?'

Frau Kiegerl was thoughtful. 'Not so much hurt or let down, but disappointed — yes. The women who chase him he — ' she gestured with her hands, 'plays with, flirts with, but when he finds a woman he is really attracted to she looks the other way. Fashionable, sophisticated women, the type Robert finds appealing, like city life. They may have some interest in horses, but not in pigs and growing crops or fish — or even making money. They only want to be a baroness. That would not suit Robert,' she laughed impishly. 'He is in the prime of his life, Angela, and, like his father, a virile man.'

Angela felt her cheeks turning pink. She was quite sure that Robert would not appreciate his mother talking about him in such a way, even though what she said was true.

He was a worker, often doing manual labour, as he was the type of man who would not delegate his staff to do things he was not prepared to do himself. He had a superb physique, one which readily suggested a man with a healthy sexual appetite.

Angela turned back to the guest list, reading out the names and placing their bedroom number by the name as Frau Kiegerl chose the appropriate rooms.

One name at least was familiar to her — Andreas Klug.

'A veterinary surgeon from Graz,' Robert's mother explained. 'And these Fräuleins . . . '

'Erika Wolf, Lottë Winkler and Maria Müller,' Angela recited.

Frau Kiegerl groaned. 'Too many women — but — if he chooses only one it makes the other two jealous, and gives cause for the chosen one to think she is special to Robert.' She banged her stick down on the floor. 'Ah, *mein sohn, mein sohn.*' She stood up and took Angela's arm again. 'We should have an even number of men and women — but it must be Robert's choice, and he likes to be surrounded by beautiful women.' The old lady looked at Angela fondly. 'When they see you, my dear, they'll want to — ' and she shaped her hands like claws, 'but you take no notice. You're younger than they are and your beauty is fresh.'

Angela laughed. 'But I'm only Robert's secretary.'

Frau Kiegerl squeezed her hand and muttered something in German which Angela did not catch. She wasn't looking forward to the weekend, but at least she now knew what she was up against — a bevy of glamorous women all craving to become Baroness Kiegerl!

There was some satisfaction to be gained from making the necessary arrangements. Robert was a good organiser and spared nothing in the interests of his guests.

After lunch the following day Robert hovered about in the office, finally saying: 'I have to go into Deutschlandsberg. I think you must come with me, Angela.'

'Yes, of course,' she said eagerly, thinking he needed some assistance, but for a moment he seemed reluctant to say what was on his mind.

'I would like you to wear our national costume during the weekend. All Austrian women wear it for such occasions, and I will be happy to buy it for you as a present. I'll take you to the shop and introduce you then while you are being fitted I have business at the bank.' He spoke rapidly as if he expected her to be offended.

She certainly was!

'I am English,' she stated defiantly. 'More so than Austrian, and I think your local people wouldn't like to see me taking such a liberty. I have quite suitable clothes to wear for your party.'

She was trembling with indignation. No man, certainly not her boss, was going to dictate what she was going to wear!

3

'You are as much Austrian as English. You will look well in the costume,' Robert said. 'You will offend no one — only me if you do not agree. I am trying to be generous, Angela.'

'Patronising,' Angela replied shortly. 'First you order me to remain here over the weekend to help your mother, which I'm happy to do, except that I would have preferred to be asked, and now you insult me by telling me what to wear. Perhaps you wish to make it clear to your guests that I'm merely one of your staff. Well, you can do that without dressing me up in national costume. I'll just stand at the door and receive hats and coats.' She switched her typewriter on and began typing furiously.

'Your pride does you credit,' he said sarcastically. 'If you behave like that at the weekend my guests will see you for what you are — a frustrated spinster secretary. You will please the fräuleins, they will think I am losing my touch with the only woman I need tolerate, apart from my mother.' He stalked out of the office banging the door so fiercely that the office shook, as if in sympathy with Angela's trembling frame.

She hid her face in her hands. Why did she antagonise the man so? What he had suggested wasn't so awful. She would have willingly complied if his mother had asked her. Not that she needed a costume bought for her. She already had one, made only a year ago by her mother. It was hanging in the wardrobe of her room at her uncle's farmhouse.

Angela stared at the schedule of activities she was supposed to be typing. Horse riding, fishing in the lake, tennis, shooting for the men, she knew it off by heart. It was the thought of the other fräuleins which bothered her. They would all be dutifully wearing national costume. Why couldn't she do the same to please Robert? That was what she really wanted to do, but she was afraid of the competition. And now Robert had put her in her place. He saw her as the only other woman he need 'tolerate' apart from his mother. That was unkind. His mother was sweet-natured and devoted to Robert — too much so perhaps.

At least he would have all the stimulation he needed over the weekend. Angela doubted that he would ever try anything on with her again. He'd only made a pass because he thought it was expected of him, probably. Now he knew that Angela wasn't going to fall at his feet and worship him, he'd leave her alone.

That thought did not make her feel any better. She had to try to be amenable or she would surely lose her job and that would mean going home to face Christopher and the girl who had taken her place.

She spent the remainder of the afternoon getting lists, menus and place cards typed and tried to visualise all the events which were planned. Her temper cooled, and she felt ashamed of her unyielding manner over the costume. It was only Robert's pride which was hurt. All the same, she felt she ought to make amends. She telephoned Josef at her uncle's farm.

'About the weekend, Josef,' Angela began.

'I've seen Robert and told him I would like to join in as many activities as I can. Didn't he tell you?'

'He hasn't been in the office this afternoon.' She went on to explain about the incident with Robert over national costume, and asked Josef to get his mother to pack her outfit up for him to bring with him on Saturday.

After ringing off, she placed the letters to be signed on

Robert's desk and left the office.

She found Frau Kiegerl in the small sitting room.

'Shall I leave these menus and things with you just to look over?' Angela asked.

'I'm sure they're perfect, Angela, but I'll check them over if it makes you happier.'

Angela went off to get ready for dinner, dreading a further confrontation with Robert, but apart from nodding a greeting across the table he ignored her, and as soon as he had finished eating he excused himself and left the room. Angela expected Frau Kiegerl to mention the matter of wearing national costume, but nothing was said so she presumed Robert had not told his mother of the incident. She wished he had. She would like to have discussed it with someone just to ease her mind.

As the time drew nearer for guests to arrive, Angela had little time to think about her relationship with her boss. From midday work in the office ceased, and while Frau Kiegerl rested Angela checked the bedrooms.

Extra help had been enlisted from the village, and Angela decided to go and get ready. In the hall she found Lilli with a strange man talking to Robert.

Lilli came forward to greet Angela, kissing her fondly on both cheeks. 'Angela, you are looking prettier than ever. This is Rudolph, my husband.'

The man talking to Robert broke off and turned to Angela. He was tall and distinguished, his hair mid-brown, his complexion fresh with grey-green eyes that lightened with a smile as he shook Angela's hand. Somehow Angela knew he was exactly right for Lilli. They made an ideal couple.

'So, Angela, you are being thrown in at the deep end,' Lilli said. 'You've hardly had time to get used to life at the hall and here you are coping with a house party. Robert's a very lucky man.'

'So I keep telling myself,' Robert muttered, and only

Angela could appreciate the sarcasm, although when she dared to glance at him she saw that his expression was one of amusement.

'Is everything ready? I hope Mama hasn't been overdoing it,' Lilli said.

'I've tried to see that she hasn't,' Angela said. 'She's resting now.'

'No, I'm not,' came a voice from the gallery. Rudolph rushed up the stairs and kissed his mother-in-law.

They were evidently a close-knit family; no wonder Frau Kiegerl was concerned about Robert's choice of partner. Whoever he chose, she would have to be prepared to share him with his mother and sister.

It was evident that Robert and Rudolph were good friends too. Only Angela was an outsider. They did their best to include her, but she felt too English to be a part of this family.

Robert and Rudolph carried the cases up to the bedroom and Lilli tucked her arm through Angela's as she made for the opposite staircase.

'What are you going to wear, Angela?' Lilli asked.

'I don't have that much to choose from — not here,' Angela explained. 'Would you like to come to my room and see if the dress I've chosen is suitable?'

Angela was pleased to get Lilli inside her room behind the closed door where she could tell her that Robert had requested her to wear national costume.

'I'm only half Austrian,' she explained. 'I don't want to offend anyone and anyway I haven't got it here with me. Josef will bring it over tomorrow.'

Lilli smiled. 'How like Robert,' she murmured, more to herself than to Angela. 'It was his way, my dear, of trying to make you feel like one of the family, and that's a rare concession for Robert. But you wear whatever makes you feel comfortable.' She went to the back of the door where a dark red dress was hanging on a hanger. It was made of jersey silk with a cross-over bodice gathered into small yokes at the shoulder and a skirt made up of numerous narrow pleats.

'It's lovely, Angela, suits your dark colouring. I hope you're going to enjoy yourself.'

'I do feel rather like an intruder.'

'I'm sure Mama would be very unhappy to hear you say that. It's true, she is not always easy to get on with, but she has taken to you, so you must not let her hear you say that you feel like an intruder.'

'I didn't mean it in an offensive way, but I *am* only Robert's secretary.'

'Only?' Lilli laughed. 'To Robert and Mama that is a position of great importance! Now I must go and get dressed. We'll talk later, Angela.'

Angela laid a hand on Lilli's arm to restrain her. 'Please, Lilli, I would rather you didn't say anything to Robert about me wearing national costume.'

'You are going to surprise him at the barbecue? — I like that,' she said with a chuckle as she left the room.

Angela felt happier having spoken with Lilli, such a warm, friendly person. She possessed that rare quality of putting people at their ease, and was one who could be counted on to give sound advice and ready help.

As Angela brushed her shoulder-length dark hair she surveyed herself critically in the mirror. Her dress complimented her figure and gave her confidence. A few minutes later she was standing beside Robert in the great hall being introduced to his guests.

Angela was sure she would never remember their names, but Dr Weiss, Frau Kiegerl's friend, was easy to identify, being much older. There were three other married couples besides Lilli and Rudolph, and a tall blonde-haired woman, whom Robert introduced as Fräulein Erika Wolf.

Angela's smile was met with austere appraisal.

'English!' the older woman observed.
Robert quickly explained who Angela was while Fräulein Wolf never took her gaze from Angela's face.
'An English secretary — now there's a novelty, Robert *liebling*,' she said, without glancing at him.
Angela felt frozen by her cold stare.
'Pretty too,' Erika Wolf observed drily, 'but then you always did have an eye for beauty.'
'My secretary, Erika, as you should remember,' Robert said crisply, 'does not need to be beautiful.'
'No, *liebling*, just a willing slave — as your pretty little English miss will soon discover,' she added cryptically.
Angela presumed that this was one of his past employees.
The house seemed full of people. Refreshments had been served on the patio outside the large drawing room, which was decorated in a shade of pale green. The upholstery was striped in green and gold brocade, the rest of the furniture expensively antique, bearing witness to the wealth and standing of the Kiegerl aristocracy of a bygone era. Angela was impressed by it all, also overawed.
Early arrivals had taken their refreshment and returned to their rooms to unpack and dress for dinner. Rudolph and Dr Weiss were strolling in the garden in earnest conversation. Angela went to one of the tables on the terrace and felt the teapot.
'The English must always have time for tea,' a female voice said at her side, and she turned to find a round, rosy-faced girl about to place an empty cup and saucer on the table. 'Let me introduce myself — Lotte Winkler.'
'How do you do?' The girl's friendly warmth made Angela feel at ease at once. She was shorter than Angela and plump, her ample bosom accentuated by the low-cut blouse of the Steiermark costume. The niceness of her personality was written in her face and her beaming smile.
Angela laughed at her quip about the English and their tea.

'You evidently like the habit too,' she observed. 'I'm Angela, by the way, Robert's secretary.'

'I know, I've heard all about you, Angela.'

Angela raised her eyebrows in surprise. 'But I've only been here a short time.'

'I know that too — but Robert's secretaries always encourage much speculation.'

Angela hesitated before asking, 'You wouldn't be an ex-secretary of his by any chance?'

'No. I met Robert years ago in London. We studied English together before I came home to medical school. I am a doctor you see.'

'A very good one,' Robert said, coming up behind Lotte and placing his arm around her shoulder. 'Busy too, so it is a great honour for us to have her company. We are going to have a great time, aren't we, Lotte?'

Lotte looked up at Robert. Her large dark eyes, almost as black as her hair, sparkled as if in fond memory of past intimacy.

'We all expect to enjoy ourselves,' Lotte said, then glancing at Angela went on, 'Robert and his mother — Lilli and Rudolph too — are perfect hosts. If anyone does not enjoy themselves then I think it must be their own fault.'

'And what do you think of my new employee?' Robert asked Lotte.

'I think you should ask those questions when I'm not present, Robert,' Angela said.

'You are a very clever man, Robert,' Lotte said, again looking up into his eyes with more meaning than her words expressed.

'Mm,' he agreed, 'I think so too. Come, *liebling*, we will walk in the garden and I will tell you all about her.'

Angela felt like one of his prize animals — something he'd just bought at market with which he was well pleased. She poured a second cup of tea, half cold, and watched them as they sauntered off, arms around each other, across the wide expanse of lush green lawn.

So much for Robert and his beautiful women, Angela thought. Lotte was very pleasant but quite a homely girl. It had come as a surprise that she was a qualified doctor.

Eva came to clear the outside tables and Angela helped her. More wine — that was served at any time of day — was placed on the terrace and in the drawing room, and many of the guests strolled round the garden sipping an aperitif. Angela was happy to sit on the stone balustrade which spanned the patio. It was a perfect evening, the sun reluctant to set although the moon was already out. A light, gentle breeze fanned her cheeks and made the leaves of the shrubs rustle in the stillness. A distant trickle of water came from the fountain in the ornamental goldfish pond. A beautifully sculpted bird was the centrepiece of the fountain. Was it a stork, or a flamingo? Angela, no ornithologist, couldn't be certain, but whatever it was it was exactly right.

A rippled of female laughter drew Angela's attention to a couple in the distance. Were these the women Robert's mother spoke of? No one could find fault with a happy-go-lucky girl like Lotte. Erika Wolf was a different proposition altogether — the sophisticated type whose beauty might attract Robert, but not his mother.

There were still two guests whom as yet Angela had not met — Andreas Klug and Maria Müller. Perhaps they were coming together. Since Andreas Klug was to occupy a single room, he was presumably unmarried.

But when everyone was seated around the long dinner table, Andreas Klug still had not appeared. Fräulein Maria Müller, the last to arrive, was a tall, slim, shapeless woman with a frosty expression — frosty that is except when one of the men in the room spoke to her, whereupon she bubbled with uncharacteristic animation.

It was like Christmas, Angela thought, with delicious

courses being served one after another and wine flowing freely. Light, frothy Viennese desserts with lashings of fresh cream were tempting but Angela could manage only one small helping. She was glad that on this occasion Robert was sitting at the other end of the long table, with Erika on his right and Maria on his left. Dr Weiss was Angela's neighbour and the empty seat which Andreas should have occupied was immediately opposite her. There was lively conversation to accompany the meal, some incomprehensible to Angela. As she sipped the smooth white wine, she caught some snippets of conversation about herself from the far end of the table. Robert was repeating what he had said to Angela, that as she was so young she would soon be homesick and would return home.

Angela placed her empty glass on the table and glared at him. 'I think you are being premature, Robert,' she said. 'I don't feel homesick in the slightest, and I have no intention of returning to England for quite some time.'

'Bravo, Angela,' Frau Kiegerl cried, and the other guests made approving noises, welcoming her stated intention to remain in their country.

Robert remained unconvinced. 'I know Angela better than any of you, and I repeat that the call of her homeland will become too great to be ignored, and I shall be the one to be sorry.'

The general babble started again, most of the guests teasing Robert about his secretaries, both past and present.

'Home, my dear, is wherever you are happy, and I hope you will be happy in our beloved Austria,' Dr Weiss said to Angela. He was an endearing man, with a wise and fatherly manner.

Coffee was served in the drawing room. Robert was missing, and Lotte chatted with Angela until he returned and came over to Angela.

'Angela, Andreas has just arrived. I wonder if you would keep him company while he eats, and then bring him here to join us?'

Angela went with Robert — she could hardly refuse — but she was aware of a knowing smile exchanged between Lotte and Robert.

Andreas sat down at the dining-room table while Robert pulled out his mother's chair for Angela, at his place before leaving the room.

'Thank you, Angela,' Andreas said after she had greeted him. 'I'm grateful to you for sparing some time to sit with me.'

'I'm sorry you were held up — not trouble with transport I hope?'

Andreas smiled at her. 'No — I have a sturdy English Range-Rover, which I need to visit isolated farms. Today, though, I was in the Alps to help a cow which was sick.'

Angela had forgotten what work he did. 'Oh, of course, you're a vet,' she said.

At first he looked puzzled then with a laugh said: 'That's right — *Tierarzt* — veterinary surgeon.'

'In England we'd say this was a busman's holiday,' Angela said, 'coming to stay on a farm.'

Andreas regarded her with his keen blue eyes. 'But I haven't come to see the animals,' he smiled. 'It's the human element I'm interested in.'

Angela lowered her gaze, well aware of what he meant.

'Robert's house parties are usually most enjoyable,' he went on, 'and give me a chance to ride, which I can't do in Graz, and play tennis.'

'I love tennis,' Angela enthused.

'Good — you'll be my first partner.'

Angela knew — had known from the moment she had first set eyes on him — that she liked Andreas. He had a certain gallantry about him; when they returned to the drawing room, he never left her side and was quick to find her a seat or fetch her a drink. For the first time she was made to feel like a guest.

Sixteen was about the right number for such a party, Angela decided. Quiet, intimate conversations were possible, but so was general conversation.

Robert's voice was usually the loudest, especially when he laughed — which he did almost all the time that he and Lotte were together. Now he was speaking generally.

'Angela,' he called, looking round the room for her, 'I hope you've got a notebook on you.'

She looked puzzled, 'Hardly,' she said, at which everyone laughed.

He walked slowly across the room to where she was standing with Andreas.

'We shall have to get our riding event organised,' he said.

'Angela and I will be playing tennis,' Andreas told him.

'You can ride first,' Robert argued.

'I can't ride,' Angela intervened.

Robert looked down at her with some exasperation. 'Then we must teach you,' he said.

'But I don't wish to ride a horse,' she insisted.

'I don't have any camels,' he replied irritably. 'Of course you must ride. Supposing I'm away in the fields and you have a message for me?'

'I'll have to find someone who can take it to you,' she said with a shrug.

He gave her a severe look, then smiled at his other guests. 'Whoever heard of a secretary on a farm who can't ride a horse?' He shook his head in mock dismay, then added, 'It is no great problem — Angela *will* learn to ride.'

In the laughter which followed only Andreas heard Angela mutter under her breath 'Angela will *not* learn to ride.'

He placed his hand round her waist and whispered, 'Don't worry, I'll look after you.'

At that moment Erika slid to Robert's side and, placing a hand through his arm, crooned, 'I always carry a notebook, Robert *liebling*, as you know. No good secretary should ever be without one.' Her flashing eyes triumphed over Angela who managed to bite back an angry retort. What sort of person attended a party carrying a notebook and pencil?

Robert shrugged and laughed, though without much humour.

'It's all right, Erika. I'm sure Angela won't mind going to the office for hers.'

Andreas held Angela firmly, swinging her round and out of the drawing room before she could protest. He guided her across the hall and through the arched oak door which he closed behind them. As soon as they reached the office Angela switched on the light and pulled free to go to her desk drawer.

'Angela — a chance to be alone together. Let's make the most of it,' Andreas whispered.

'But Robert's waiting,' she protested in surprise.

'Then let him wait. It isn't right that he should make you work when there are more exciting things to do.'

With gentle hands he drew her close, until his lips could easily reach hers. His kiss was persuasive yet lacked passion, so that Angela responded mildly. Vague doubts crossed her mind as to what kind of house party this was supposed to be. She couldn't believe that Frau Kiegerl would allow a 'change-partners' game under her roof, yet there did seem to be an undercurrent of unrest.

Occasionally she had found herself at a 'change partners' party with Christopher. She'd never liked it. She had felt too possessive of Christopher, for one thing. Now, though, she was free — yes, really free — to take whatever opportunities turned up. She liked the idea of having a protector like Andreas, but she must not become too involved. Tomorrow Josef would expect to partner her.

'I think our absence will be noticed,' she pleaded at last, but Andreas held her head in his hands and looked long and lovingly into her eyes. His blue eyes mesmerised her with their almost mystic gaze. His skin was fair, perhaps too delicate for a man, and his lips were finely drawn lines in his boyish face. But the expert touch as he brushed her eyes, nose and cheeks showed the skill of an ardent lover.

He slid his hands down her back and clasped them together at her waist. His gaze wandered down her throat, resting briefly on her crystal pendant, and she knew he was impatient to explore what lay beneath.

He held the jewel in the tips of his fingers and was pressing it back against her skin when they heard the outer door bang.

Angela jumped, but Andreas seemed not to be worried by the approaching footsteps. He caught her mouth between his lips, this time with frightening intensity. She tried in vain to draw back. He held on, crushing her body against his, the intimacy of his kiss straining every nerve-end to the limit.

'So,' Robert's loud voice boomed, 'my secretary is being exploited.'

When at last, Andreas released her, Angela emerged from his clasp hot and breathless.

'Work first, Angela, *meine lieb* — the nights are for loving,' Robert scolded.

'She couldn't find her notebook,' Andreas excused light-heartedly, but Robert went straight to the drawer in her desk and held it out to her, his dark, challenging eyes boring into hers.

She might almost have enjoyed the interlude with Andreas. She knew there was more to come — he had staked his claim on her from the moment he had arrived — but Angela was remembering Robert's kisses. Kisses of fire, and a declaration that she would do his bidding be it making notes or satisfying him in bed. In the hostility which darted like an arrow between them Angela realised that he was reminding her of his expectations.

She pretended not to notice and took her notebook meekly. Andreas was still clutching one of her hands. She glanced at him, pleading to be released, but the two men were deep in muttered conversation.

Angela was confused. She couldn't make out the implications yet it was as if both men were perfectly content with the situation. She wished she could feel the same. For Robert to discover her in Andreas's arms gave her a feeling of guilt. But hadn't it been Robert who had introduced them? Hadn't he picked her to socialise with Andreas?

They were obviously close friends, and Angela wondered if they had made a bet on which one would conquer her. You flatter yourself, my girl, she reproached herself. There had to be some ulterior motive though, to explain their reactions.

'It will take no more than a few moments, Angela,' Robert said persuasively. 'If you would just make a list of the horses we shall require in the morning, the grooms will have them ready.'

As Robert dictated the horses' names and the suggested riders, Andreas left the room.

Not everyone would be riding, but Robert included Andreas and added, 'Your own name, of course, Angela — I think Bari will be a nice little horse for you to start on.'

Angela felt her nerves tighten with impatience. Couldn't the man understand plain English! She tapped her pencil on the notepad.

'I'm sorry, Robert, I don't seem to have made myself clear. I don't ride,' she said flatly.

Robert was pacing round in circles in his usual way. Now he walked slowly towards her. He was wearing an immaculate dark brown suit with a peach-coloured shirt and dark brown silk bow-tie. His thick dark hair was groomed in crinkled waves, almost but not quite curling over at the ends. He was so . . . so large, so dominant, so bronzed . . . She thought ridiculously — what a perfect specimen he would make as a Herculean statue.

He sat on the edge of her desk so that his face was level with hers. With awesome calmness he took away her notebook and pencil and threw them across to his desk. Then he took her hands in his and stared deliberately at her.

'Are you afraid?' he asked in a low voice.

'No! Well, yes, I suppose I am,' she admitted. 'I'm a town girl. I like the farm and the country, but that doesn't mean I want to milk cows and drive a tractor — or ride a horse.'

'You are like all the others, you want to be a city girl here in the country.' He shook his head sadly. '*Meine lieb*, couldn't you try to adapt — just for me?'

Was he really pleading with her, or was he mocking her? It didn't matter . . . She knew in that instant that she wanted him to draw her into a tender embrace. Yes — he had changed in that disarming way of his into a gentle, considerate man. Yet she liked him best when he was fierce — not violent, but aggressive, and eager to manipulate her.

He didn't touch her though. Instead he studied her carefully, his eyes assessing the outline of her figure. Andreas had toyed with her pendant, now she willed Robert to do the same. She longed to feel his fingers against her skin. They would be direct in their approach, irresistible in their quest.

Angela took a step forward, almost unconsciously, and Robert immediately stood up so that he towered above her.

If she leaned forward just a tiny bit she might almost hear his heartbeat. She wanted to, desperately, but there was a strange reluctance dividing them. Slowly she lifted her eyes to his dark brown ones.

'*Liebling*,' he said softly and, with a smile, 'Better in English, I think — *darling*. The nights are for loving, Angela, and,' he added cruelly, 'Andreas will be waiting.'

He dropped her hands and Angela was forced to step back feeling suddenly very empty. But when she reached the door he called her back.

She turned. He was holding out her notepad.

'Spare me from Erika — *bitte*?' She sat down and uncovered her typewriter. Thoughts rushed through her head, questions which needed answering, and yet her throat seemed to be constricted that she couldn't utter a sound.

He stood behind her until she had wound the paper through the machine. She felt his hand on her back. It sent a dart of expectancy through her. He bent down and kissed the side of her neck. Not gently, nor cruelly but firmly enough to make her feel helpless. As he pulled at her skin, playing on the sensitivity of the area, she felt her strength flowing out of her.

'I had better return to my guests,' he said huskily, 'or they will wonder what we're doing. You can leave the list on the table in the hall. I'll see that Ludwig has it first thing in the morning.'

Angela felt she had drawn some compassion from him after all. He had, in the end, accepted that she wouldn't ride, even if he had humiliated her in front of his guests. That was Robert's way. She paused to rub her neck. It was a little sore, but she liked the feeling. There was much more meaning in his actions than in the gentle flirtation of Andreas.

4

Suddenly she was eager to be back in the drawing room. Wasn't it nice to be thought of as one of the family rather than a guest, she mused, as her fingers tapped lightly over the keys on her typewriter.

She soon completed the list for the stables and, leaving it in the hall as Robert had instructed, she pushed open the drawing-room door. Soft music was coming from the speakers, a Strauss waltz, lively yet romantic and one or two couples were drifting lazily about. You could hardly call it dancing, she thought. With a little misgiving she noticed Lilli in the centre of the room with her arms around Andreas's neck. Robert was across the room on the far side, his back to Angela as he talked earnestly with Erika and Maria, while Lotte was seated on a couch keeping Frau Kiegerl company. Angela felt a touch of envy that Lotte was so completely at home at the Baron's hall. She seemed so natural, so at ease, so perfectly attuned to the atmosphere, so right a choice to be the next Baroness Kiegerl. She must be nearing thirty, Angela judged, perhaps even older, but her round happy features, ebony hair and bright eyes made her look much younger.

'You look wistful, Angela; a little mystified too?' Rudolph pushed a tumbler full of wine into her hand. She looked up at Lilli's husband thinking that he should have been a film star — there was a definite look of James Stewart about him. 'Just wondering who everybody is,' she admitted.

He began to explain about some of the guests. The

married couples were mainly landowners from the neighbourhood. Before he could turn his attention to the single women, Lilli and Andreas joined them.

Lilli looked up at Rudolph; Rudolph looked down into his wife's eyes and Angela recognised that they understood each other so well they had no need to speak. Without a word they merged together, Rudolph elegantly tall and lean, Lilli much shorter but very beautiful, hardly able to link her arms about Rudolph's neck as they moved across the room.

Andreas followed Angela's gaze. 'A charming couple . . . '

'A marvellous union — two very special people,' Angela said, still watching them with admiration. 'They must have been married for some years yet they love each other completely.'

'You sound envious,' Andreas said.

'Who wouldn't be? In these days it's rare to meet two people who are not afraid to show the world how much they love each other.'

'Your time will come, *meine leib*. You are young. Sometimes it is better not to fall in love too soon. If you have lived an exciting life, met lots of people, then it will be a lasting love.'

Angela found her gaze drawn from the ideal couple to Robert. He looked as if he would like to move, but Erika and Maria were unwilling to let him go.

'You are wondering why Robert did not also find such a love when he was younger?' It was as if Andreas could read her mind.

'He's a wealthy, good-looking man with a title,' Angela conceded. 'I'm surprised someone hasn't snapped him up.'

'No one will ever "snap" Robert up,' Andreas said with a laugh. 'Many have tried — are trying still as you can see — but Robert is a determined man, obstinate his mother thinks. He should be married, of course,' Andreas went on positively. 'He is thirty-six years old. Like his sister he fell in love — how d'you say — head over the heels — at twenty-one when he was in England.'

'What happened?' Angela asked in surprise.

'She wanted him, but only after she had done all the things she wanted to do first — got her professional qualifications, travelled to various places — making sure, as she said, that she wouldn't meet someone else she loved more.'

'How callous,' Angela said. 'Her feelings must have been very shallow.'

'I agree with you, but Robert was blind for a long time and would not see her for what she was. Now he tends to be suspicious of women. A great pity, for he is a good man and should be married.'

Even as Angela watched Robert's broad back muscles eddying beneath his shirt in rhythm with his laughter, he stepped back from his lady friends and gradually sidled towards the couch where his mother and Lotte were still chatting.

Andreas halted the track of Angela's thoughts as he set aside their glasses of wine and eagerly gathered her in his arms. He twisted her around the floor, but over his shoulder she could still see Robert, Lotte and Frau Kiegerl.

She had an idea that Lotte was the girl he had loved. Angela wanted to despise her for treating him so shabbily, even more so for coming back into his life to torment him. Of course he loved her still — it showed in every look, every action. And Lotte — what were her emotions? Was it her career which had come first? Was she too ambitious? Dedicated to the work she loved so that Robert was destined to come second? That wouldn't do for Robert, Angela knew. His standards for marriage would have been set by his elder sister.

Andreas twirled her gently round again, his lips nuzzling her ear, but Angela did not respond. She wanted to observe Robert.

He and Lotte were helping his mother towards the door. Angela felt a pang of resentment: it was usually she who went upstairs with Robert's mother.

Frau Kiegerl called a general goodnight and the little party of three left the room, but almost immediately Robert returned. His eyes met Angela's and he raised his eyebrows in mock reproof. For what, she wondered? This was just a social occasion when people played games with each other. There was no harm in such casual behaviour: it meant absolutely nothing. Andreas was comforting though. He cared about her feelings, and showed more interest in her than Robert did.

Andreas was teasing her neck. Angela tossed her hair back and laughed as he slid his fingers into her black silky tresses. Over his shoulder she saw that Robert was holding Maria close as they circled the centre of the floor slowly. They were talking earnestly but Robert was holding himself stiffly. There was no sensuality in his body now. Maria was slight and Robert's masculine strength made her look frail.

Some time later, when Andreas and Angela were sitting down sipping their wine, Robert escorted Maria to the small couch where his mother had been sitting, and left her with Dr Weiss. Then he went to Erika and, although Angela couldn't see too well, she felt sure he had placed both hands on her knees, squeezing gently until she stood up. Being rather tall, she was able to hang on to Robert's neck as they went into a clinch. Erika was a classic beauty, a great volume of smokey-blonde hair swirled round her head, and her figure was sensationally good. Her black dress clung in all the right places. Robert was evidently pleased to have such a fine feminine form in his arms. Angela watched as his fingers slid to the slender curves of Erika's back and hips. It seemed obvious that he liked his women mature. Erika was certainly that, but her expression was not pleasant and her rather small, shrewd eyes were cold.

Angela would have liked to dance with Robert — if only so show him that her attachment to Andreas was merely casual. But Lotte returned, and Robert soon enclosed her in his arms with great zest. Angela felt exasperated. If all that Andreas had said was true how could the man be such a great softie! Lotte saw no future with Robert and yet he still craved her love. His admiration of her was open; anyone could see that his appreciation was genuine. Angela felt her cheeks flush with embarrassment as Robert moulded Lotte's plumpness to his own big, hard body.

'It's rather hot in here,' she said, standing up suddenly. 'I think I'd like a breath of fresh air.'

Andreas took her hand and they skirted the dancers to reach the terrace. Maybe it was the wine going to her head. She was no great drinker and usually had difficulty in getting through one large glass, but she did not want to offend the Austrians, who drank wine like water.

As they lingered at the foot of the terrace, footsteps brought a figure to the top step. He looked massive silhouetted in the night air against the glow of light which streamed from the open doorway.

'A busy day tomorrow, Angela,' Robert called gently, with a touch of irony in his voice. 'I wouldn't like you to be locked out.'

Andreas answered in some colloquial phrase that Angela didn't know — something about being a spoilsport — and they sauntered round the goldfish pond. Angela, though grateful for the fresh night air, was soon shivering.

'It is not good to go from such a warm temperature to a cold one, *meine lieb*,' Andreas said. 'I think perhaps it is time to say goodnight.'

Angela agreed. A weariness had come over her, and she

let Andreas escort her back to the drawing room, where everyone was preparing to retire. The married couples were wending their way upstairs. There was no sign of Lotte or Maria, and Dr Weiss had already departed.

Andreas locked the french windows and Angela murmured goodnight. Robert answered curtly and Angela felt slightly bemused that Erika had remained behind with him.

Erika met Angela's glance with undisguised glee. Her feline eyes held a look of victory as she said, 'You're brave, staying up so late when you have a lot to arrange tomorrow. Sleep well, Fräulein.'

'And you, Fräulein,' Angela replied tersely, and hurriedly left the room to get away from her hostile rival.

Andreas caught her up on the stairs and Angela wondered how she would shake him off, but at her door he cupped her face in his hands and kissed her tenderly.

'Goodnight, *meine schöne liebchen*. I will ride with the party in the morning, and afterwards we will play tennis.' He kissed her again with a little more feeling and then strode off along the corridor.

As he disappeared she felt a moment of disappointment. She couldn't be sure why. Did she really want him to force his way into her room and probably take it for granted that he could stay the night? She liked him well enough, she felt she had a friend, but beyond that she was not prepared to go — unlike other members of the party, she realised as hushed voices drew nearer. Angela opened her door and stepped inside, but she did not switch the light on for a moment. Instead she peeped out again in time to see Erika, conspicuous by her light hair, arms entwined with Robert's as they sauntered along the passage. The sound of the door closing softly echoed along the corridor and everything became still.

* * *

Lying in bed, she thought over the events of the day. Lucky Robert to have three women to admire and spoil him, but why go to bed with Erika — if he had — when he was so obsessed with Lotte?

She recalled Frau Kiegerl's words, how these women who wanted Robert so badly would get their claws out when they saw his new English fräulein. Now she knew that Frau Kiegerl must have been referring to Maria and Erika. But they would hardly regard this particular English secretary as a threat to their relationship with the man they wanted. Angela decided that they didn't pose a threat to her either. *She* was Robert's secretary. He had chosen her, met her once and then singled her out to offer her the job. Why, she wondered, had he a vacancy when Erika seemed to be so keen on the job still?

However much she tried not to imagine what was going on in Erika's room she found it impossible to put the lovers out of her mind. An image of Erika's model figure came to her in the darkness, and the thought of Robert's skilful hands raking over her voluptuous body tormented her. His bronze, Herculean torso would be lying naked beside that of his mistress. Was he loving her with tenderness, or was he satisfying his lust with little thought for her feelings? Was he making passionate love to Erika while the woman in his mind's eye was Lotte? It was a distressing thought that he could be capable of such mental cruelty.

But thank goodness he had Erika and Maria, so that he didn't need Angela as his next mistress!

If only Lotte would go away, get out of his life for good, perhaps in time he would meet a woman whom he could trust enough to marry. How that would please his mother, and Lilli too! He needed a woman with the same generous warmth as his sister. Someone who would love him, who would teach him how to love in return without this mad craving to take a woman merely as an exercise . . .

* * *

Next morning Angela felt heavy-eyed, but what was the use of her worrying about her boss and his social entertaining? It meant nothing to her. She should be pleased that he was leaving her alone, she scolded herself, as she sat down with coffee and a roll.

It wasn't so easy to view the situation in that light though. He had threatened to take her to bed. Was she just a little bit peeved that he had chosen someone else? Someone he'd known before, someone well experienced in how to respond in the art of love-making. What would he expect of her, she wondered? Wasn't it better for her to remain inexperienced to keep herself pure for the man she would marry one day?

The smell of leather made Angela aware that Robert had entered the breakfast room. He came to sit beside her, and she was forced to meet his smouldering look.

'Angela,' he questioned, 'have I put too much responsibility on you this weekend?'

She stared blankly at him. 'No,' she answered at length, shaking her head.

'Mama says you look tired. You are pale. Are you well?'

Now his meaning dawned on her and she blushed more deeply as she shook her head again. These foreigners were so bold! Even intimate biological functions were discussed openly, and the reasoning behind his question became more obvious when he added:

'I came to see if I could persuade you to change your mind and come riding? The others have left already. I would take you with me — give you your first lesson — but I did not think — perhaps today you — in English, I think you say have a headache?'

She felt like melting away under his scrutiny. Not so much with embarrassment as with surprise at his considerateness. His warm brown eyes embraced her, for a brief moment she felt that she and Robert had the same emotional union as Lilli and Rudolph. She seemed to be drifting away on a heady cloud of romantic fantasy.

'I don't ride, Robert,' she said calmly, reassuring her self-control. 'Not today or any other day, although in reply to your kind inquiry, I'm perfectly well.'

Robert lifted his hand in a hopeless gesture and she almost relented and begged him to teach her to ride.

'Then I must see to it that you have lessons before our next house party,' he said. He got up abruptly and stalked off in his normal arrogant manner.

For a moment he had shown a little sympathy, shown that he could be considerate and knew how to treat a woman at the time when she needs delicate handling. But having established that Angela was not in that condition, he had quickly reverted to his aggressive manner.

Frau Kiegerl and Dr Weiss joined her. 'Your uncle does not keep horses now, I believe?' Frau Kiegerl asked.

'No.'

'And in the town it is not easy to follow country sports?' Dr Weiss added wisely.

Angela smiled in agreement. By the look on Robert's mother's face, she was being labelled 'another town girl flirting with the country'.

If she was going to stay here — and she was, wasn't she? — she was going to have to make an effort to fit in with farm life outside the office.

She excused herself from the table and went back to her room, where she changed into her short, white tennis dress. It had a V-neck which, like the short sleeves, was trimmed with emerald green.

When she heard the clip-clop of horses' hooves she picked up her racquet and hurried down to the courtyard. The riders were coming in two or three at a time. Andreas jumped down and greeted Angela cordially.

'Hello, Angela. You are ready and waiting for me?' he said.

'There was nothing else for me to do so I thought I

might as well,' she answered, a little perturbed by the possessive kiss which Andreas planted at the side of her mouth.

Lilli passed them and said, 'If I can persuade Rudolph to be so energetic we'll come and join you for a game of doubles.'

'Did Rudolph ride?' Angela asked. not seeing him anywhere.

'No, he prefers walking and fishing,' Lilli answered. She set her horse off across the courtyard towards the stables.

'I'll go for a quick change but first, walk over to the stables with me — yes?' Andreas invited.

A groom came to take the horse, but they lingered a while as other riders returned. This was Angela's first visit to the stables. She found the huge animals rather daunting by their sheer size, but with Andreas gently introducing her to them in turn she became less nervous.

'You have never ridden?' Andreas asked her. Angela shook her head. 'Robert must give you time to gain confidence with the livestock on the farm,' Andreas suggested kindly.

'I feel as if I've been here ages,' she said, 'but so far I've only seen the office, part of the house, and the garden.'

'I suppose Robert thinks you aren't interested in anything beyond the paperwork. He runs a good farm, though. After lunch today he'll take his guests on a guided tour, that's why there are so many staff here making the place extra clean. But it is not really necessary — Robert is a most conscientious man. You must join the party.'

They wandered back to the house, meeting Robert and Erika returning, deep in conversation. 'Why don't you come for a game of tennis?' Andreas called, but Robert waved his hand in a negative gesture and rode on.

Angela waited in the hall for Andreas until he came running down the stairs looking boyish and ebullient in white shorts and cotton shirt.

They went through the garden to the tennis courts. At first they played for fun, warming-up games, but when Lilli and Rudolph joined them it was hard, vigorous play and Angela showed her expertise by helping Lilli to beat the men.

After lunch, when Robert led the party on a conducted tour, Angela and Andreas brought up the rear. She hoped Robert hadn't noticed that she was there. His concern earlier had probably only been at his mother's instigation, and Angela knew he was losing patience with her. She'd refused his offer of national costume, she didn't ride, and as Andreas was treating her as his chosen partner, it was not surprising that Robert preferred to ignore her.

Had Robert hoped for a deep involvement with her by now in order to make the older women jealous? The thought was a flattering one — but Robert was a law unto himself. During normal working hours he might find it amusing to tease his English fräulein, but Angela knew she was no match for the likes of Erika and Lotte.

Angela's attention was soon absorbed by the farm. They visited the piggery, the cowsheds, and the immaculately clean milking parlour. She could hear Robert at the head of the party, the volume of his powerful voice echoing back to her quite clearly.

The tour ended at the fish farm, on the opposite side of the road to the house. It was evident from the pride in Robert's voice that he was pleased with this venture, and indeed everyone was intrigued with the shoaling masses of lively speckled trout.

While one of Robert's staff explained the layout, Angela drew level with Robert. He showed surprise at her presence.

'I suppose you don't understand much of this,' he said, 'but Klaus cannot speak English, unfortunately.'

'I understand most of it,' Angela protested.

'The best way to learn any language,' Andreas said, 'is

by living among the people who speak it. In a year, Robert, Angela will be as fluent as we are.'

Robert laughed sarcastically. 'By then she will have decided she doesn't like us after all, and will be safely back in England, I think.'

Angela shot him a hostile look thinking that she didn't particularly like him at that moment anyway, and moved on, leaving Andreas and Robert to be as derisory as they chose about her future.

When they returned to the house Angela was delighted to find Josef on the terrace, where tea and coffee were being served. There were delicious pastries and cakes, Viennese specialities all laid out temptingly.

'Especially for Angela's benefit,' Robert announced, 'we have English afternoon tea.'

'I am honoured,' she quipped.

'Not really,' he said in a lower tone. 'I like afternoon tea and I think it's an English custom we should adopt.' He turned to Josef and the two men ambled off, discussing farming matters.

After tea a few of the men went back to their fishing, leaving the women to chat or rest and then to change for the evening barbecue. This, Angela learned from Frau Kiegerl, was not only for the benefit of family and guests, but was also Robert's tribute to his employees for a good harvest. They were all invited, and Angela's offer of help was firmly refused.

Angela was wearing the denims she had changed into after tennis. Robert, to her surprise, had shown no sign of disapproval. Now, as she was walking through the wood with Josef, he ran his hand familiarly over her thighs and bottom.

'I wish more Austrian girls would wear tight clothes,' he teased.

'Then you're in the minority, Josef. I'm sure Robert thoroughly disapproves.'

'I think you do not understand your employer, Angela,' Josef said seriously. 'Robert is a much sought-after man. He is very fond of women, especially young and pretty girls, which is why *I* shall be looking after you.' He gave her a playful squeeze — she supposed it was only meant to be a playful one.

She knew she should count herself lucky to have two such nice men paying court to her, but however nice Josef and Andreas were, it was mostly Robert who occupied her thoughts. She tried to tell herself that it was because he was her boss, and as she didn't want to jeopardise her job it was important to try to please him.

Josef led the way among the trees to a secluded hollow, where lights were hanging from tall poles and sausages and steaks were sizzling over a charcoal fire, sending out an appetising aroma in the dusk.

Angela exclaimed at the sight of everyone dressed in national costume, the men in grey suits with a wide green stripe down the trousers and the same green trim on their jackets, symbolic of the West Steiermark.

'Did you remember?' she asked Josef anxiously.

'Of course! Your skirt and blouse are folded in a bag on the back seat of the car. My mother saw to it all.'

'Good, then I'll go and change, but don't tell anyone where I am.'

The costume suited her. The short-sleeved white blouse with its low, scooped neckline, topped with a fitting waistcoat in light blue, showed off her figure, and over the red patterned skirt she tied a darker blue apron. Round her neck she wore a dark blue velvet choker with a sparkling brooch at her throat. She brushed her hair until it shone and, as if to add some gypsy magic, applied make-up more liberally than usual.

Returning through the drawing room she came upon Frau Kiegerl and Dr Weiss.

'My dear — you look enchanting,' Robert's mother

said. 'Now tonight you are truly a girl of the West Steiermark.'

'I'm proud to wear it,' Angela said shyly. 'My mother made it, so I am wearing it for her.'

Frau Kiegerl caught hold of Angela's fingers. 'Your mama would indeed be proud of her daughter, but . . . I think she would like to see a smile of happiness.'

'But I am happy, Frau Kiegerl,' Angela insisted.

'On the outside, yes, but on the inside? Ah, Angela, my dear, I am an old woman, and wise in such things. Your turn will come, but you must be patient.'

Angela laughingly pulled away and ran towards the hollow.

The musicians had arrived: she could hear folk music played by the local accordion band some time before she reached the party. Everyone seemed to be enjoying themselves, and Angela was eager to see how Robert would react to her dress. She hung back until there was a lull in people going to him for the food he was cooking and then she went forward and stood beside him.

'Can I help?' shs asked softly.

'My secretary should be doing that,' he answered absent-mindedly, and then, as recognition dawned, he stopped turning the steaks and looked directly at her.

There was a long, embarrassing silence while his brown eyes darkened and his eyebrows came down in a heavy frown. 'So you think you can cheat me with your independence — eh?'

Angela had never heard him speak with such acidity before, and when Erika appeared at his other side, linking her arm solicitiously through his and whispering in his ear, she turned and crept away feeling as if she had been whipped.

5

Tears of misery threatened, but she bravely warded them off and went to sit on a bale of straw close to where the musicians were playing. A few moments later Josef and Lotte came to share her seat.

'You have nothing to eat,' Lotte said in surprise.

'I'm . . . not hungry yet.'

'But you must eat and drink,' Josef said, and before she could stop him he had gone off, returning shortly with a plate of pork cutlets, green salad and a roll, as well as a glass of wine.

At least as she ate she was spared the ordeal of having to make conversation, but when Andreas joined them and sat close to her, placing a comforting arm round her shoulder, she felt calmer.

There was some happy folk singing but Angela could only pretend to join in, her spirits were so low. She had wanted to please Robert, instead she had angered him. She couldn't understand it. He'd been the one to suggest she wore traditional costume, but what was the point in buying it when she already owned one.

She wanted to go to him and explain, but either Erika or Maria was constantly at his side. Josef and Andreas must have sensed her unhappiness because they soon had her dancing, and insisted she ate more of the delicious pork. Angela never ceased to be amazed at the amount of meat Austrian people ate, but tonight she was unable to do justice to the feast.

The evening dragged on. At any other time Angela

wouldn't have wanted it to end, but Robert was ignoring her and she couldn't believe how much it hurt. Eventually the singing became more sentimental, the fire died and the local people began to wander off to their homes.

Josef said he too must leave. 'My parents like to go to church early on Sundays,' he said, 'so I must be up for milking. But father will do the evening turn so that I'm free to take you out.'

'Will you be coming over here tomorrow?' Angela asked as she strolled towards the courtyard with him.

'Robert has invited me to take part in the fishing and to stay to lunch. I know that Andreas has taken a liking to you, Angela, so I won't intrude.' He kissed her swiftly and added, 'I've promised to see Lotte tomorrow.'

Angela could see Josef's eyes gleaming with animation. Now was her chance to ask him about Lotte.

'Did you know Lotte before today?' she queried.

'No, but I like her very much.'

Angela opened her mouth to tell her cousin what Andreas had told her, but Josef held her close to him and kissed her lightly.

'I don't have to worry about making you jealous because we're cousins, and I know how lucky I am to have a lovely cousin like you. See you tomorrow, Angela.'

He got into his car and drove off into the night. She remained where she was, listening to the sound of his engine as it grew fainter. She pulled her black woollen shawl round her shoulders. In the stillness of the valley she could hear muffled voices from the guests in the drawing room. Then another noise broke the tranquility. From the direction of the barns beyond the stables she heard the rumble of a tractor.

Curious, Angela made her way back towards the hollow. It was eerie at the edge of the wood, especially when all the lights went out in the hollow below her. Soon afterwards the tractor began to move forward, chugging its way slowly up the bank towards the track.

As the tractor made it to the top, the figure driving it looked round to make sure the trailer would clear the bank. It was Robert. On a sudden impulse Angela ran and jumped up on the bales of hay on the trailer.

The tractor came to a standstill inside a shed where a solitary light burned over the door. She heard Robert switch off the engine, and when nothing happened for a moment she panicked, thinking he might not unload but go away and lock up the shed, leaving her imprisoned. She jumped off the trailer just as Robert reached the back of it. He uttered a savage oath and gripped her shoulders angrily.

'Robert,' she began tremulously, 'I — '

'What are you doing still up?'

'I thought you might need help — and — '

'And what?' he demanded ruthlessly, making her feel weak beside him.

'I wanted to explain,' she said.

'In the middle of the night?'

'You never give me time to talk to you properly.'

'Go on, Angela,' he said in a husky voice, quite different from his savagery a moment before. 'I'm listening.'

'I . . . I want,' she stammered without daring to look directly at him, 'I mean, I feel I ought to apologise. It was very kind of you to offer to buy my dress for today but I already had it. My mother made it for me over a year ago,' she explained hurriedly. 'It was at my uncle's farm, Josef brought it over today.'

'So why could you not have told me before?'

His face was large and close. He looked dangerous as he bent lower to hear her reply.

'I . . . I don't know. You take everything for granted, Robert,' she said, meekly twisting her fingers round the tassels on her shawl.

'And you, Angela, are taking this for granted, I imagine.'

He crushed her slim body hard against his as his mouth wantonly consumed hers. She struggled wildly, trying to kick him, but he wheeled her round and her feet left the ground as he lifted and flung her down on to a bed of straw. She opened her mouth to protest but he silenced her with his tongue which was like a flame setting her alight. There was a primitive impetuosity in his actions, a faint odour of wine on his breath as his kisses tore her apart.

She could feel no unbearable weight pressing her down, only a hardness against her thighs. She pushed against his shoulders and from deep inside her, her voice screamed silently in agony. But Robert was at his skilful best when resisted. He laughed roughly, caught her hands and splayed them on the hay above her head. Holding her helpless, he gazed into her eyes, his own a mirror of Satanic cruelty as his lips brushed hers, pecking, biting, nibbling below her chin down her throat, round her neck below her choker, along her shoulders. Now he held both hands in one of his so that he could slip her blouse over one shoulder.

'No, Robert, no!' she implored, but he went on relentlessly exploring, holding one exposed breast and kissing it in a fever of passion. Then, as if checked by the tender youthfulness of her body, his intensity subsided, his caresses became gentle, his kisses more controlled.

'Angela, *meine lieb*, now you will admit that being my secretary is better on my terms.'

'I didn't wait for you for this, she cried in a trembling voice as tears pricked her eyes. 'I wish I'd gone to bed.'

'And missed the fun?' he mocked, still urging his body to excite hers.

'I told you once before that you're a maniac and you are,' she cried. 'You've got three mistresses, what do you want, a harem — all to do your bidding?'

He laughed and slid his large hands down to her waist, squeezing gently. 'Why should I need more mistresses when I pay you to do the job?' he whispered seductively.

She lifted her hands to strike his cheek. He caught and held it, but in an unguarded moment she managed to steer it close to her mouth and bit his hand viciously.

He jerked back. 'You will not do that again, *fräulein*,' he said fiercely, and for a long dangerous moment Angela was left wondering how he would retaliate. 'Get to bed before I — '

He let her go and she ran with all speed across to the terrace, her breath coming in painful gasps that burned her throat as she entered the house.

In the safety — was it safe? Would she ever be safe from Robert now? — of her own room she thought she must have awakened the entire household, but no one stirred.

She was in bed when she heard the tell-tale click of a door opposite. Tonight Robert was evidently sleeping alone.

Angela realised that he could just as easily cross the passageway, but somehow she knew he wouldn't. At least she had shown him that she was willing to fight, and he had said that he was tired. Not too tired for that! she thought with disgust.

As she relaxed she slid her cool fingers down the length of her body, a body which was defying all her innocence with a new-found curiosity. She wondered what it would feel like to have him tease and delight her senses with only this sheer nightdress between her skin and his. Her own reactions shocked her. She had never felt that way over Christopher, and although Andreas's advances were suggestive, she knew that no one would gain her submission as easily as Robert.

He's an older, more mature man, she told herself firmly. When he ignored her she felt wretched, when he tormented her she played hard to get to salve her conscience. All the time she loved him to excite her with his aggressiveness.

In the cold light of day her mind behaved more rationally. She thought she was the first one down for breakfast until Lotte emerged from the kitchen carrying a tray.

'Hello, Angela, you're early. Frau Kiegerl is going to have breakfast in bed, on my orders, then I'm going to church with Maria. Will you come?'

Angela hesitated. 'I usually go with my grandmother and aunt,' she said, 'but I think I'll give it a miss today. There may be things to do here, and I *am* Robert's secretary after all.'

Actually Angela couldn't bear the thought of having to go and confess those sinful thoughts concerning herself and Robert. They were exhilarating during darkness, but now she felt only guilt.

She was pouring coffee at the sideboard when she heard the front door slam, and Robert's heavy tread brought him straight to the breakfast room.

'Good morning, Angela,' he said, his voice booming.

She replied courteously, but went to sit at a wrought-iron table on the terrace.

After a few moments he suddenly appeared at her elbow, making her jump. She spilled the coffee she had been in the act of drinking.

'*Meine lieb*,' he said with concern, 'what's the matter? You were not afraid of me last night.'

'I'm not afraid of you now,' Angela retorted, getting to her feet and shaking out her apron. 'You made me jump. I didn't hear you coming.' Coffee was trickling down her chin and into her cleavage. She hastily found her handkerchief and started to mop it up, angry that it had stained her white blouse. Robert took the handkerchief from her fumbling fingers. He made great sport of exploiting her accident, his fingers lingering inside the neck of her blouse. Gazing fondly at her, he willed her to look up at him, and when she did, anger and mistrust melted away. She knew he was going to kiss her, but she was not prepared for the sweet ecstasy she felt — nor for the sarcastic feminine voice from the doorway.

'What a splendid way to start the day,' Erika sneered, 'or are you still continuing from last night?'

Robert slowly, damnably slowly, severed the connection between his lips and Angela's, and continued the mopping-up exercise unconcernedly, while Angela's cheeks burned uncomfortably.

'Why not, Erika? If it's good there's no point in stopping,' Robert said smugly. 'What is the English cliché? Strike while the iron is hot?'

'Someone might get burnt,' Erika warned in a mocking voice.

Robert laughed heartily, and to Angela's humiliation held up his hand which clearly showed some teeth marks.

'Someone already did,' he said with a knowing look at Angela, as if to say that she would get paid back for such a crime.

'*Liebling*,' Erika crooned, moving closer, 'I do believe those are teeth marks. Not human teeth, I hope?'

Robert's gaze didn't flinch from Angela's burning eyes.

'Only a kitten,' he said in a warm, sensuous voice. 'Just a playful kitten.'

'I didn't know you had cats here at the farm,' Erika said innocently.

Robert gave Angela a wink as he explained: 'One of the workers on the estate owns a cat with a litter of kittens. I've taken a couple of them — they help to keep down the vermin.' He handed Angela her handkerchief. 'Not any damage done I trust, Angela?'

'I'd better go and change,' she murmured, looking down at herself.

'What *have* you been doing?' Erika smirked. 'Someone else nearly got burnt I see,' and she clicked her teeth in disapproval.

Robert smiled at Angela, silently telling her to take no notice.

'It was my fault, wasn't it, *liebling*,' he said. 'You should have let me buy you a blouse after all, you see. The stain is hardly noticeable. Please keep it on. I think our traditional costume suits you.' He turned at last to Erika. 'Have you had breakfast?'

'Of course. I've been up hours, I thought you would have been up early too.'

'I'm always up at six, as you know.'

How did Erika know, Angela wondered, unless she spent some intimate nights with him.

'The men have been fishing for two hours,' Robert divulged. 'Why don't you join them, Erika.'

The tall girl sighed and cast a suspicious glance at Angela. 'I suppose I might as well — oh, by the way, Robert *leibling*, is it all right if I stay on for a few days?'

'Certainly,' he agreed graciously, then added, 'But I shall be going away mid-week. I have to visit Vienna, the usual autumn conference, but you can stay and keep Mama company if you like.'

Erika looked put out. 'Mm — I'll just stay for a couple of days then. Of course, if you want company in Vienna?' she offered hopefully.

'It's a business trip, Erika,' Robert answered quietly. 'Now, if you'll excuse us we'd like some breakfast.' He went back to the kitchen.

In a contemptuous tone, Erika said to Angela, 'Robert never keeps a secretary longer than three months you know, *fräulein*.'

'Yes, I do know,' Angela replied sweetly. 'I don't mind. I shall be ready to go as soon as he tires of me.'

75

Erika swung round and made for the front door. Angela knew she had been rather naughty to goad Erika, but Robert had done so too by letting Erika think that Angela was following the pattern that Erika herself perhaps had set for Robert's secretaries. It was all too much for Angela to understand. No wonder he didn't marry when he could have female company just for the asking, and in the space of a weekend had chosen to co-habit with Lotte, then Erika, and now Angela. No, he hadn't been to bed with Angela, though she didn't doubt for one moment that he would have if she had issued an invitation. But however tempting, she didn't want to go that far.

'Come, Angela,' Robert said, returning with a tray. 'Breakfast on the terrace.'

'But I only wanted coffee,' she said.

'Nonsense. I insist that you keep me company.'

Actually she was glad of the opportunity to sit and talk with him quietly. They sat opposite each other as they usually did when guests were not present, and Angela felt a comforting sense of togetherness. She was aware of his muscular arms; he seldom wore his sleeves down to the wrist and she guessed that the watch on his left wrist was solid gold. For a working farmer his hands were elegant, well-groomed with good manicured nails. He exuded stamina, a powerfully built man with strength to match that of his animals.

Now she was finding it easier to look straight into his eyes, even when he was not wearing spectacles. He pushed his plate aside, and as he did so he stretched out his long legs so that one of them knocked her knee under the table. She waited for him to apologise but he didn't. Instead he kept on moving his leg against her knee until she was forced to look up at him. He leant his brawny arms across the table in front of him and grinned devilishly.

'We won't hurry the terms of my contract,' he said meaningfully.

'I haven't got a contract,' she argued. 'And anyway it's hardly worth bothering as I'm only going to stay for three months.'

As she picked up her cup to drink her coffee she felt his hand on her knee. 'Stop it, Robert,' she pleaded. 'I shall spill it again.'

'Let me help you,' he suggested flippantly, tipping the bottom of the cup.

They both began to laugh. If only he were always like this, she thought, and then from across the table he asked: 'Is Josef coming today?'

'Yes, to see Lotte, and as she's gone to church I rather think Josef might meet her there.' She didn't mean to make it sound clandestine but immediately Robert's face clouded. Was it with jealousy, pain, or disappointment? A long silence followed and for once Robert seemed to be ill at ease.

'You don't mind?' he asked at length.

'Mind? Why on earth should I? Josef and I are cousins. We enjoy one another's company, but I would be as pleased as Uncle Franz and Aunt Hilde if he could find a girl he wanted to marry.'

'Ah — Angela, if only life could be arranged that easily. Love and marriage are for the very young, I think.'

'And is that why you prefer the idolatry of your ex-secretaries?' She knew she was annoying him, but this seemed a good opportunity to discuss the things which puzzled her. He pursed his lips and ran his long fingers through the mass of tousled black hair.

'My secretaries are a joke, Angela. You must not take this thing so seriously. Maria was with me for a few years and she was an excellent secretary, but she had to go back to her village to care for her elderly parents. I invite her here to give her a break from her arduous duties.'

'And Erika?' Angela pursued daringly.

He did not answer, reverting to the subject of Josef and

Lotte. 'But Lotte is a doctor, you know. I hope Josef will realise that she is dedicated to her work, which would hardly be compatible with a farmer's life.'

Angela's breasts swelled with compassion for Robert. How he must have loved Lotte. All this frivolous talk, his clownish behaviour and passionate advances were perhaps his way of combating unrequited love. Angela was consumed with sympathy and would have willingly given up all her principles to let him take some of his frustration out on her. Only from pity, she vowed, but looking across at the tormented brow, the straight, honest nose which helped to form his strong handsome features, she saw in a flash that he was too proud to use a woman for such a purpose.

'They have only just met, Robert,' she reminded him, and he smiled in agreement.

'That is true, Angela, but they tell me there is something called love at first sight.' He banged his hands down on the table indicating that he had talked enough, then stood up. 'You will please bring a notebook, Angela, and we will go across to the lake to see who has caught the largest fish.'

Angela looked down at herself. 'I think I ought to change — this looks bad,' she said pulling at the front of her blouse.

'Only because you know it's there. It really doesn't show.' He grabbed her hand and led her to the office where he pushed notebook and pencil in her hand.

When they reached the lake the anglers were packing up. Gradually, they all made their way back to the hall. Wine was now being served on the terrace so Angela escaped to her room to change.

She was beginning to feel more like one of the family. She asked Eva if there was anything she could do to help, but the middle-aged housekeeper shook her head then stood back and admired Angela's appearance.

'*Schone fräulein!*' she said with approval, meaning too that Angela must not work in such finery.

Robert entered the dining room at that moment to check on the preparations for the last meal for his guests.

He actually raised his eyebrows in appreciation.

'A most appealing *fräulein*,' he said. 'Going somewhere, Angela?'

'Josef did suggest taking me back to the farm with him this evening to see my grandmother.'

'He and Lotte have just arrived. Perhaps I should warn you that you may be disappointed. I have a suspicion they have other plans which might not include a third person.'

'I don't mind,' Angela said.

Luncheon was a jolly affair, enhanced by good wine and excellent food. It started with *leberknodel*, small liver and herb dumplings served in meat soup, then came the main course of *tafelspitz*, beef cooked in wine served with vegetables, and this was followed by delicious *apfelstrudel* and cream.

It was easy to see that Lotte was as besotted with Josef, as Josef was with her. Josef and Robert, Angela thought, and her heart ached for both men. If what Andreas had said was true, Lotte was likely to be only playing with Josef's affections just as she had done with Robert's. What she cared most about was her career. Yet Angela wasn't entirely convinced. Lotte had realised her ambition. She *was* a doctor. Perhaps now, at around thirty, she was ready to settle down and have children of her own.

Angela glanced along the table to where Robert was sitting at the end, Erika on one side, Maria on the other. Two very beautiful and sophisticated women, Angela was forced to admit, and yet really, she believed, he loved the warm, homely Lotte.

After lunch, Angela found herself included in a drive up into the Alps to a coffee and ice-cream house of high repute. Robert, his mother, Lilli and Rudolph stood in the courtyard to wave everyone goodbye. Lotte and Angela got into the back seat of Josef's car, and with Andreas sitting in the front they set off.

Looking back, Angela noticed Erika's jubilant expression as she linked arms with Robert. Frau Kiegerl turned to go back into the house.

The remainder of the day passed pleasantly and Angela was able to relax in the company of Josef and Andreas. Lotte too was great fun to be with, but Angela was unable to discover any details about her other than that she worked in the children's department of a new, modern hospital in Graz.

'I'll take you there and we'll get Lotte to show you over the whole hospital,' Andreas suggested.

This was after an evening meal at a country hotel; they were on their way back to Kiegerl Hall.

'Do you know Graz?' Andreas asked Angela, whom he held in a firm embrace in the back seat.

'A little. Josef has taken me there once or twice.'

'You will come into Graz one day with me,' Andreas promised, then kissing her cheek and nibbling at her ear he whispered, 'A weekend — how would you like that? I'll show you round our city.'

'If Robert let's me have a weekend off,' Angela whispered back.

'You usually go to visit Josef and his family at weekends I believe? Perhaps he will come to Graz to visit Lotte, and would bring you with him?'

'That would be nice,' Angela agreed.

Angela supposed Andreas was being prudent, to allow Josef and Lotte's relationship to develop a little more. She was glad for Josef. Happiness radiated from him, as it did from Lotte.

They returned late. From the courtyard, which was in darkness, Angela noticed the office light on. Could Robert be working? She remembered that Fräulein Erika Wolf was still a guest. Were they together in the office? Was Erika doing Angela's job?

Angela led the way into the house where they found Frau Kiegerl sitting by the fire in the small sitting room with Erika. Almost at once Robert joined them.

Supper was offered, but everyone agreed that they had eaten well, so Andreas, Lotte and Josef said their goodbyes and Angela stood with Robert to watch the cars move off.

Simultaneously Angela and Robert turned towards the front door together. Robert held out his arm and Angela moved willingly into its embrace.

'Well, *meine lieb*, have you enjoyed your outing?' he asked. 'You and Andreas playing gooseberry with Josef and Lotte? Or was it the other way round?'

Angela found it so easy to slip her arm round Robert's waist comfortingly.

'No one was playing gooseberry,' she assured him happily. Robert was leading her towards the front door to the office, which was on the east side of the main front door. 'Don't tell me you've been working?'

'Why not?'

'Surely your mother and Erika would have liked your company?'

Robert sighed. 'Everyone needed to rest, Angela.' He smiled at her. 'Only the young have energy to go on enjoying themselves. Mama will be ready to go up now.' He looked at his watch. 'Already ten-thirty, but she would not go to bed until her new charge was home.'

'You mean me?' Angela asked in surprise. 'I'm sorry, Robert, I didn't think. I mean, she knew I was with Josef and Andreas. She doesn't usually wait up for me when I go to the farm.'

'True, but tonight she was anxious to see you return.'

'I expect she wanted to say goodbye to Lotte and Andreas,' Angela said, 'but I'll go and help her.'

Robert restrained her. 'There's no need. Erika is with her.'

Angela's face fell. 'Of course,' she said penitently.

Robert pulled towards the office as they went in through the entrance, and with one arm still round Angela's waist he closed and bolted the main door.

'I shall be going to Vienna, Angela, on Wednesday, so, as Erika is staying on until then. I've asked her to help you in the office if she's at a loose end.'

'Oh, Robert,' Angela said in dismay, 'I wish you hadn't. I don't like — ' she stopped herself.

'You don't like Erika?'

Angela looked down. For a few magical moments she had felt so close to Robert that she might almost have imagined they were in love. How stupid, she reproached herself, and how thoughtless to voice her opinion of his other woman, his ex-secretary, lover, or whatever he chose to call her.

'I . . . I'm sorry, Robert,' she said in a low voice, keeping her eyes averted. 'I mean, I'm sorry that I can't like Fräulein Wolf — if she's special to you.'

He moved slowly towards her. She watched his large shoes spanning the distance between them just like a slow motion film, while she clutched at her purse in front of her. She was obliged to glance up under fluttering eyelids as the toe-caps of his brogues met the toes of her black sandals.

Then, still in slow motion, his face advanced towards hers. She knew that her heartbeats had quickened, were now racing and thumping against her chest as her eyes invited, begged, and implored him to kiss her. His lips touched hers — once, twice — slow but devastatingly enticing kisses, and then with one gentle hand he held her chin firmly, forcing her to gaze straight into his lovely but wicked brown eyes.

'There's only one woman who's special to me, *liebling*,

at the moment, and that is my present secretary.'

She would have fallen against him. She wanted more of those exciting kisses, she wanted to hug him, and be hugged. In that instant she knew that the whole world could go on revolving because she loved Baron Robert Kiegerl with a frightening intensity which she had never before experienced.

A shuffle of impatient footsteps could be heard hurrying through the stone-flagged passageway.

'*Liebling*, aren't you *ever* coming to bed?' said Erika.

The magic evaporated. Angela turned and rushed past Erika, along chilly corridors, through the warmth of the hall, speeding up the stairs, her mind flooded with bitter regrets.

6

Angela threw herself down on her bed and wept. The ache inside her was more than she could bear. She'd half hated, half loved her boss, in a meaningless kind of way. Now she wanted him so desperately, despite all his clowning and his idle flirtations, with an emotion that went far deeper.

She would never be able to to on working for him now. How could she hide this new-found knowledge? The deep pain of it must surely show. Tomorrow she would tell him. Not that she loved him — wouldn't he just laugh at her, a mere slip of a girl, and he a mature man? No, there was only one way to get out of this situation — to say she wanted to go home. Let him attribute the change in her to being homesick for England, not lovesick for him.

This lovesickness for a man who would never love her was far worse than any homesickness for England could be. He had loved once so deeply, a love which had been spurned, so now he simply looked to women to satisfy his virile need.

Angela lay in the silent darkness going back over the weekend. It had been a good party. She recalled the obvious affinity which Robert and Lotte had showed at the start... Then Josef had arrived and Lotte had allowed Erika to monopolise Robert. Did Josef know of the relationship Angela suspected between Robert and Lotte years ago?

She felt envious of the devotion between Lilli and Rudolph. She had always thought that being in love should be like that. Tears of misery spilled from her long, dark lashes until sleep came as a blessed relief.

She slept remarkably well and woke with a feeling of exuberance which she could not explain. Was it that she really was homesick and eager to return to England?

She was up and dressed by seven-thirty and found Robert already eating his breakfast. She greeted him cheerily. That instant she decided that she did have the courage to stay and work for him after all — and to love him secretly.

'Good morning, Angela,' he said, glancing up from his plateful of bacon and eggs. 'You're up early. I thought you would have slept on after the busy weekend.'

'It's a lovely morning, I was awake so I thought I'd make an early start — you said there's a lot to do before you go to Vienna.'

'I shall be working in the wine garden while the weather is good. The grapes must all be gathered in now. There are one or two things I would like done in connection with my trip to Vienna, but Erika has offered to help.'

Angela felt sharply deflated, and Robert evidently noticed the change in her. He went on, 'Erika used to work here. I haven't been able to give as much time as I would like to show you your duties, so now is a good time to have expert tuition.'

Angela couldn't look at him openly, but her expression betrayed her feelings.

'Erika really isn't that unbearable, *meine lieb*, and it will ease the burden for Mama,' Robert explained.

Angela cringed. So Erika was staying in order to supervise the office in Robert's absence. A whole week? Would her nerves stand all that hostility?

After breakfast Angela began the daily routine. She was glad to sit at her typewriter and release her frustration through her fingers flying over the keys.

Robert came in later with Erika. For the first hour or so Erika worked without speaking to Angela. Then the interruptions began. Erika took it upon herself to answer the telephone, and embarked upon lengthy familiar conversations with most of the callers. Angela had been Robert's secretary long enough now to be known also, and it was obvious from Erika's remarks that many of the callers enquired about her. As the day wore on Erika grew more impatient with these enquiries, and when the farm manager called in and went straight to Angela for the information he required, Erika looked exceedingly put out.

'I suppose the minute the bad weather comes you'll be packing your suitcases to go home to England?'

'I haven't any such plans, *fräulein*.' Angela spoke calmly, disguising her resentment at Erika's hostile tone.

'Like most young people I imagine when you get tired of the quiet country life you'll be off.' Erika went on.

'Is that why you left?' Angela was surprised at her own boldness. A stony silence followed. Then Erika shattered her dreams.

'There's not too much secretarial work to do during the winter months,' she said. 'Robert usually goes up to the mountains ski-ing, so don't be surprised if your employment is terminated by Christmas.' Erika delivered this information with great relish. She laughed. 'Don't be fooled, *fräulein*. Your beloved Robert may have a certain fondness for English girls, but he would never marry one.'

Angela opened her mouth to deny ever having considered such a possibility when Erika continued, 'His wife will have to drive, ride, ski, swim and keep up with all his activities. He expects perfection, and none of us are that.'

Angela answered softly, 'I'm only Robert's secretary, and so far he doesn't seem to have many complaints. I wouldn't presume to be anything more than that.'

She typed the last envelope then switched off the machine and covered it up. 'Shall I leave these with you, *fräulein*?' she asked sweetly.

Erika indicated that Angela should put the letters on the corner of Robert's desk. 'No, I am not working on,' she said emphatically. 'They'll be up at the wine garden until dusk. Now I suppose we shall have to go and suffer Frau Kiegerl's grumbles over dinner.'

Angela did not respond. Frau Kiegerl was occasionally critical, but she was kind and had always been agreeable to Angela. Above all she idolised her son, so Angela felt she had something in common with her.

As she got ready for dinner, Angela pondered Erika's words. What exactly did she mean by saying that Robert had a certain fondness for English girls? Andreas had said he had fallen in love at twenty-one. Robert had been at college in England at the same time as Lotte. But Lotte was not English . . .

She surveyed her wardrobe. What could she wear to impress the man she loved? But Erika had suggested he was unlikely to return for dinner until later. Her enthusiasm waned. She was a fool to love him, for he didn't love her in return. Now Erika had informed her that she was likely to lose her job by Christmas anyway. She had given up the idea of resigning immediately. She might as well stay and love him in her own way until he told her to go. What was it that Erika had said? — 'your beloved Robert'. Did she know how Angela felt? Had all the weekend guests seen it in her eyes before she recognised it herself? Could Robert be aware of her feelings? No, she told herself, a man didn't notice things of that sort.

In the dining room Frau Kiegerl greeted her warmly, holding out both her hands.

'How are you, Frau Kiegerl?' Angela enquired.

'A little tired, my dear. So many people to talk to over the weekend is a strain for a woman of my age. But, tell me, how did you enjoy it?'

'Very much, though I'm sure I didn't do all I should have done to help.'

'Nonsense, Angela. You weren't expected to work all the time. Next spring, when Robert invites some different guests, you will be more experienced, even more like one of the family.'

Next spring, Angela thought. Would she be here?

'Tell me,' Frau Kiegerl continued, 'you went out with Josef, Andreas and Lotte? Robert tells me that Josef is quite taken up with Lotte.'

'They did get on very well together,' Angela agreed.

Eva sounded the gong then, and Erika walked into the room wearing a pale pink knitted suit which fitted her voluptuous figure to perfection. She was a sophisticated beauty, Angela conceded, but it was a pity she had a cruel twist to her mouth.

Erika went to help Frau Kiegerl out of the chair, but the old lady banged her stick down hard on the parquet flooring.

'You mustn't spoil me, Erika,' she said adamantly. 'I'm not an invalid, you know, even if I am getting frail.'

Was there some hidden antagonism in her voice? During the meal Angela sensed a note of friction and she got the distinct impression that Robert's mother was none too fond of Erika Wolf.

Erika excused herself as soon as the meal was finished, so Angela accompanied Frau Kiegerl into the drawing room. Some time later Robert appeared on the terrace with Erika. They didn't come inside. In earnest conversation, they walked down the steps and on to the lawns. Erika pushed her arm through Robert's.

Frau Kiegerl banged her stick angrily, making Angela jump.

'That woman!' she complained. 'Always trying to get her claws into my son. I'll not have her for my daughter-in-law! She'll not be the next Baroness if I have anything to do with it.'

'Do you think Robert loves her?' Angela dared to ask.

'Indeed he does not!' She leaned across and patted Angela's knee. 'Forgive me, my dear. She's the sort of woman who makes me angry. I don't know why Robert invites her here. There's a streak of the devil in him. He doesn't want her, he doesn't love her, but he goads her on.'

Angela laughed in an effort to console Frau Kiegerl. 'You sound quite fierce,' she said with amusement.

'Don't let her rule you, Angela,' the old lady advised. 'She'll try to make you look bad in Robert's eyes, so be careful. She's vicious and spiteful and I'm angry with Robert for inviting her to stay on.'

'Oh, but he didn't,' Angela defended him. 'I'm sure she asked if she could stay.'

'Is that so?' Frau Kiegerl said slowly, as if something had just dawned on her. 'So, maybe Robert does know what he is doing after all.'

Voices could be heard approaching and Frau Kiegerl shifted uneasily in her chair. 'Angela, help me up. I shall go to my room. An early night won't do me any harm.'

'But Robert hasn't eaten yet,' Angela said.

'Eva will see to that — or that woman.'

Like Frau Kiegerl, Angela had no desire to share Robert's company with Erika Wolf, so she sat and talked with Robert's mother for a while before helping her to prepare for bed, and then went to her own room to write letters. It was late by the time she had finished.

She was struggling with the zip on her dress when, after a gentle tap, the door opened. Angela would have hardly heard except that the door handle rattled noisily when turned.

Robert grinned then looked down at the handle.

'I must do something about that,' he said.

'There's no need,' she quickly intervened. 'I'm just going to bed.'

'Afraid that you won't have a warning system?' he chided. 'No one else would hear anything, Angela. The house is very old and strongly built.'

'Robert,' Angela said gently. 'I said I'm going to bed.'

He advanced farther into the room pushing the door shut behind him.

She wasn't afraid of her darling Robert, of course she wasn't. All the same there was a dark, smouldering look on his face as he walked right up to her. He must have just bathed and changed as the tang of cologne was pleasantly evident.

'There is perhaps an excuse for Mama's rudeness, but not yours,' he stated, looking down at her as she stood rooted to the spot, her hands still on the zip at the back of her neck.

'Rudeness?' she echoed in disbelief.

'Yes,' he said, then turned her round and attended to the zip, sliding it down with ease. 'Erika is a guest. The way you both chose to disappear when we came in was rather pointed. So you don't like Erika, my mother doesn't like her, but that is no reason to treat her like a leper.'

'B-but, Robert, I've been working with her all day. We thought you'd like to be alone together.' It was only reason she could come up with at such short notice.

He grabbed Angela's shoulders and gave her a violent shake.

'Why should you think we wish to be alone together? What plot is this my mother is making?'

'Plot? I don't know what you mean. Frau Kiegerl was tired. She said she found talking to people over the weekend a strain. She needed help so I went up with her.'

'I expect my secretary to be prepared to report to me on the day's work, especially as I shall be up on the hillside again all day tomorrow.'

'I thought Erika would do that.'

'Angela, my mother does not like Erika. I accept that, but she does not have to worry about me getting married. She spreads gossip about me and I strongly object.'

'It's only natural that she should want to see you marry, Robert,' Angela said kindly.

'Erika is an old friend as well as an ex-secretary. I think you could show her a little more respect.'

It took a moment to sink in and then Angela's green eyes flashed angrily. 'Why should I respect your mistress?' she flung at him. 'She doesn't like me, nor does she show me any respect. It seems to me she's jealous of any other woman who manages to get anywhere near you. Well you need not think I intend to learn how to handle you from her. Next you'll be telling me to learn how to be a good mistress from her.'

He was gripping her shoulders fiercely, but she refused to beg for mercy. His fingers dug into her shoulder-blades and gradually he propelled her back to the side of the bed. He pushed her down with savagery, then eased her dress over her shoulders and down to her feet. He tossed it on to a chair and as she fought to get up he kept her down by lying on top of her.

'Erika is not my mistress,' he gritted fiercely. 'She is not special to me — not the way you are.' His mouth engaged hers hungrily. She wriggled in protest and cried out from the back of her throat. '*Liebling*,' he crooned, 'you wore our costume to please me, perhaps now you are ready to please me in other ways.'

Her slip was up in a roll around her waist as his masterful hands slid down her scantily clad body. She pushed against him. 'Why don't you go to her?' Angela yelled.

'Because she doesn't fight me,' he said with a cruel grin. His exploring fingers were doing wild, provocative things to her senses — she laughed, cried, hysterical sounds coming from somewhere inside her, and then a moan of pleasure as his caresses became gentle, stimulating — arousing a growing desire in her.

'I shall get what I want when I've tamed you, *meine lieb*,' he whispered. His lips travelled down to the delicate white skin of her half-naked breasts and with a wicked laugh he ran his hands down the length of her body. Then, rising from her, he left the room as abruptly as he had entered it.

Angela needed to take several deep breaths before she could get up. She finished undressing and got into bed quickly, putting out the light and plunging the room into darkness.

How could he torment her like this? She loved him and wanted to be loved, but with tenderness, so that she could demonstrate her love in return. She wanted so much to please him, but he never gave her the chance. Why was she wasting her love on such a devil?

* * *

Next morning Angela resolved to be kind to Erika — in order to please Robert and for no other reason. But Erika did not come to the office.

Almost as soon as Angela started work the manager of the fish farm telephoned and asked for Robert. Angela explained that he would have gone to the wine garden, but the man was adamant that she should locate him. She left the office and ran across to the stables where one of the boys insisted that he'd just seen Robert go into the cowshed.

She found him in angry confrontation with one of his workmen. She gave the message briefly.

'One of the tanks is leaking,' she said.

'Wh-at!' Robert exclaimed with fury, and raced out, pushing her violently out of the way. She fell back and would have slithered to the wet floor if the workman hadn't saved her.

'Heavens above!' she exclaimed. 'He's in a foul mood this morning.'

The workman grinned sheepishly. She had spoken in English, but he clearly got the gist.

From then on things went from bad to worse. While Angela was on the telephone Robert stalked into the office and almost pulled it out of her hand.

'Hurry up — it's urgent,' he barked.

She made her apologies, promising to ring back later.

Robert snatched the phone, dialled, and began shouting abuse at someone on the other end. Eventually he slammed the receiver down and stomped off again, cursing.

From the window Angela watched as he made his way across the road to the fish farm.

'The kind of man you could die for, isn't he, *fräulein*?'

Erika's sarcastic voice sounded behind her.

'Not when he's in a bad temper like he is today,' Angela replied indifferently.

'Seeing him as he really is perhaps? You will now fall out of love with the great master, I think.'

Angela turned to Erika. 'What makes you think I care even the tiniest bit for him?' she asked stonily.

Erika laughed sadistically. '*Meine lieb*,' she said malevolently, 'it is written in every line of your sweet little face. But now you can see Robert for the callous man he is. You love him all you like, Angela, but he will never love you. He uses women for revenge.' Her voice broke and she turned and fled.

Angela went hot, then cold. What Erika said was true. She had come to the same conclusion. How Robert must gloat if her love for him showed as plainly as Erika said.

She went back to her desk and endeavoured to concentrate on her work but was conscious of comings and goings and loud voices outside. She tried to be forgiving. He was going to Vienna next day so naturally he would be anxious for things to run smoothly during his absence. She supposed it was a tense time trying to get the grapes in before the weather changed. She glanced up at the sky through the high window. It was azure blue and clear, and the sun was pleasantly warm for early October. She hoped it would last while Robert was away, then perhaps his troubles would dissolve. She knew she was willing the days away until next week when Erika would have departed and things would be back to normal.

The slamming of doors heralded his return. He went to his desk, throwing things wildly around until he found what he wanted, then to a file where he stood perusing some documents. Angela sensed that his anger was abating.

At length he turned. 'I have to go into town. Can I take your letters?' he asked brusquely.

'They're all here. Thank you.'

'Is there anything else we need while I'm there?'

'No, not as far as I know.'

'I shall go straight on to the wine garden afterwards. Tell Erika if she exercises one of the horses she can come up and help me up there.'

Angela nodded, feeling a pang of envy. At the door Robert turned. 'Are you all right, Angela?'

'Of course,' she answered haughtily, and turned her attention to the typewriter, ashamed that a liquid film blurred her sight.

She kept telling herself what a fool she was being. Robert uses women for revenge, Erika had said. He would go on using her, taunting, irritating, persuading until she gave in to him or, even worse, take her by force and then discard her. Erika would be waiting!

Perhaps Robert really loved Erika? If Frau Kiegerl weren't around they might have been married long before this. It seemed he was capable of hurting anyone, even Erika. But most of his revenge would be directed at an English girl because of what happened when he was young.

When Erika came in later, she said, 'Robert asked me to tell you that if you're going to exercise one of the horses you might like to go up to the wine garden to help him.'

Angela saw that Erika had been weeping, though she had made an effort to conceal it with make-up. She made coffee for them both and carried the tray back to the office.

'I expect the old lady likes you to have coffee with her?' Erika said. Angela detected a penitent note in her voice and wished they could have got along together better.

'Sometimes, but I usually get my coffee and have it while I'm working.'

'She likes you,' Erika said.

Angela laughed awkwardly, and said that it was probably because Frau Kiegerl considered her much too young to be a threat to her son.

'It's not that. She sees you as the ideal for Robert, which will probably turn Robert against you. I should go back to England, Angela, before you get too involved.' For once there was no malice in her tone.

'I have my family close by in Deutschlandsberg, Erika.' She paused a moment before venturing to ask, 'Why did you stop working for Robert?'

Erika sipped her coffee. 'Hasn't the old lady told you?'

'No.'

Erika stood up. 'She will, as soon as I'm gone. But,' she shrugged, 'shall we say a little difference of opinion.'

Much later Angela heard a horse trotting across the courtyard. She felt sorry for Erika, even more sorry for Robert. He did love Erika, she felt sure, but he wouldn't marry her while his mother was so hostile towards her. She supposed it was inevitable that they would make the most of the time they could be together. Perhaps they would go to Vienna together after all.

Angela's sympathies were with Robert's mother too. It would be impossible for her and Erika to live under the same roof hating each other.

*   *   *

Next morning, Angela was up early, but as she went downstairs she could hear voices and for a moment she hesitated. It sounded like Robert and his mother and they were speaking so angrily that Angela was afraid to go in. Gradually they quietened, and Angela went on down the stairs, her heels tap-tapping across the hall before she pushed open the door to the breakfast room. She went straight to the sideboard to get her coffee but almost at once Robert began shouting again. He banged his fist down on the table to silence his mother.

'Angela is coming with me,' he shouted, then turning to Angela, 'You have half an hour to get ready.'

'Get ready for what?' she asked.

'To go to Vienna.'

'But I can't, Robert. Not at such short notice. I need to think — my clothes — my hair needs washing.'

'You can do it all at the hotel.'

'You might have told me before this,' she said.

'I'm telling you now. Stop complaining, eat your breakfast and be ready by nine o'clock,' he commanded, and strode out of the room.

Angela looked across at his mother, who shrugged and smiled wistfully.

'Frau Kiegerl,' Angela began, 'this is impossible.'

'Nothing is impossible with Robert, my dear,' the old lady said.

7

The car was speeding along the autobahn before Angela regained her breath. She tried to remember what she had packed and, more important what she had forgotten to pack. It was hard to tell what she would need as she didn't know whether she was going just for the ride or to work as Robert's secretary, but Frau Kiegerl had suggested that she would need something dressy for the evenings.

They had hardly spoken from the time Robert had banged impatiently on Angela's door, to now, nearly an hour later. A lot had happened in that hour though. First there had been Frau Kiegerl and Eva kissing her as if they would never see her again.

'Now you take care,' Robert's mother had warned. 'You're too young to be wandering about in the city alone.'

'Mama, I shall look after her, I promise.'

And then there had been the tender, affectionate goodbye between Frau Kiegerl and Robert, with some apologies on both sides Angela guessed. It was all very touching, and then she had been hustled into the front seat of a silver Mercedes Benz. She felt like a queen — albeit a very hot and flustered queen.

As Robert drove fast along the busy autobahn, Angela began to relax, and she broke the silence by saying, 'Don't ever do this to me again, Robert.'

He didn't take his eyes off the road, but Angela felt him unbend and after a few seconds he began to laugh. He placed a hand over her knee and gave it a squeeze.

'I'm sorry, *liebling*. It was unfair of me, but it's time you had a taste of city life again. You must see a little of Vienna before the winter sets in.'

'I would have liked advance warning,' she said. 'Goodness knows what I've thrown into my case.'

'For just a few days you need only essentials.'

'But what are essentials?' she asked in exasperation. 'What am I here for? To be your secretary or — ?' She didn't finish because it sounded as if she was asking too intimate a question.

'As my secretary if you like — but most men bring their wives, and while we're talking the women like to go sightseeing. Mainly shopping and spending their husbands' money,' he added.

'Isn't it going to look odd, taking your secretary — unless of course you usually do?'

'No, Angela, this will be the first time I have taken my secretary.' He paused, and when she glanced across at him, she saw that he was smiling. 'I think I shall be the envy of all my colleagues.'

'You can make it plain from the outset that I'm not that kind of secretary,' she informed him thickly.

Her tartness seemed to amuse him, but then by way of compensation he said, 'Don't worry, Angela, we have separate rooms. I telephoned the hotel last night.'

'I thought you were out all night,' she snapped. What a childish thing to say and how furious she was with herself for even showing interest.

'You waited for me to say goodnight perhaps?' Robert asked smoothly.

'No — but I'm sure your mother did.'

'Ah! Mama, dear Mama.' He fell into a thoughtful silence.

Eventually Angela asked: 'What kind of thing is this? I mean is it some organisation you belong to?'

'Mm — a conference of people interested in agricultural

developments — gentlemen farmers, you might say in England.'

Angela couldn't help giggling. 'You're not a gentleman farmer,' she taunted. 'You work much too hard.'

'Gentlemen farmers don't work in England?'

'Not the rough sort of work. They wear tweed suits, go to markets, and prod cows with their walking sticks.'

Robert laughed agreeably.

'So — you think I work too hard?'

'Your mother thinks so,' she said.

'Mama again! You must not believe all she says, Angela. I enjoy the outdoor life, though I have more incentive to work in my office now that I'm fortunate enough to have such a pretty secretary.'

'The winter is coming on, I don't suppose you'll need a secretary then.'

Robert didn't answer immediately. 'I shall still need my secretary,' he said slowly. 'I think when winter comes she will be homesick though.'

'I shall not,' she replied adamantly.

'OK, OK! Let's forget it and enjoy ourselves.'

The hotel was not in the centre of Vienna but on the outskirts, and when the car had been parked and they had signed in at the reception desk they were shown to their rooms. Angela noticed that Robert was given only one key. Had he brought her under false pretences, after all?

A young man carried their cases and unlocked the door, and as soon as he had left Robert smiled down at her.

'Only one key, Angela, but two rooms, as I said. I was tempted to book one double room, but as they offered me a two-room apartment I thought you would prefer that.'

They were in an anteroom, on one side a huge clothes cupboard and on the other a bathroom. Two doors led to the bedrooms at right and left.

'Take your pick. I imagine they are identical.' Robert opened the door on the right for her.

She was impressed by the décor — dark carpet, light wooden furniture with pale orange curtains and furnishings.

'Do you think you'll be comfortable?' he asked.

'It's lovely, Robert — and thank you,' she said.

He put her case down by the dressing table and said teasingly, 'I didn't say that I would stay in my own room all the time.'

'You came here for the conference,' she countered.

'Ah, yes,' he said ironically, 'the conference! But now I'm sure you're hungry, so just do whatever you need to do and we'll go to the restaurant, then we'll get the tour information from the desk. I'm afraid you might not have too much choice as some of the excursions finish in September.'

'I won't mind, Robert,' she assured him. 'I shall find something to do.'

'I promised Mama I would look after you.'

'I hope I wasn't the cause of your . . . argument this morning?' she asked hesitantly.

'No, Angela, only very indirectly.'

She felt she needed to make some reference to it, and even now wasn't convinced that in some way she wasn't to blame, but Robert did not elucidate and went to his own room.

Separate rooms perhaps, but certainly far from soundproof. She would always know exactly where he was and what he was doing and he would be equally conscious of her movements.

They had a snack in the restaurant as Robert promised a good meal in the evening when the conference would get under way. Other people were arriving constantly and they all seemed to know Robert. Angela discovered that he was about to be voted in as chairman for the next three years so was much in demand. It was a new and happy experience for Angela. She quickly forgot her resentment at being whisked away. She felt full of love for Robert and proud of his popularity.

The time passed quickly and at about six she asked Robert to give her the key so that she could shower and wash her hair in readiness for the evening.

She spent a long time in the bathroom, and after drying her hair she slipped into a long, elegant gown and returned to her room. Robert was sitting in the low easy chair looking at some leaflets. He glanced up as she entered. She hesitated, but he appeared to think it was perfectly natural to be sitting in her room. He looked again, his eyes raking over her from head to foot.

'You're ready so soon?' he asked.

'Heavens no,' she said, then realised he thought her gown was an evening dress. 'This is only a dressing gown.'

His dark eyes had that smouldering, wicked look. She turned her back on him and gazed in the mirror. Her own green eyes were sparkling too, but she knew she would have to ask him to leave eventually so that she could dress.

'Are you going to change?' she asked matter-of-factly.

When he didn't answer she turned to find him still scrutinising her. He smiled fondly, opened his hands to her as he whispered huskily, 'Come here, Angela.'

She hesitated, then went slowly towards him. He guided her down to sit on his knee.

'It's good enough to wear at any function,' he said.

She felt shy and spread out the soft, delicately flowered material over her knees. The gown hung loosely over her body yet not loosely enough to conceal her feminine curves. It had an elasticated waist and a three-quarter-length zip up the front which she had not fastened up to her neck.

'There is plenty of time for me to get ready,' he said. 'I thought we could work out an itinerary for your sight-seeing.'

She took the booklet of excursions he held out to her,

but she could only pretend to concentrate as his hand glided smoothly over her back and down to her thigh. His lap was comfortable and she knew that he liked to feel her close, knowing that there was nothing between her youthful creamy skin and the dressing gown. She tried not to think of how the situation might develop, though she was sure temptation was in both their minds. Such thoughts excited her and she realised the danger of the little sensuous wriggles she was unable to control, which must excite Robert.

As she opened the booklet he lowered her zip a few more inches, until the fullness of her breasts widened the opening, then down again almost to her waist. But there she laid a restraining hand on his.

'By now, *meine lieb*,' he whispered, 'you should not be shy of me. You know what I like to see and feel.' As he spoke he slid his arm round her, drawing aside her gown and taking her breast in his hand tenderly. She felt herself trying to retract both breast and nipple, but he skilfully stimulated the pink rosebud until it responded, and hardened eagerly. With his other hand he pulled the skirt of her gown up over her knees and gently smoothed her slim legs.

Angela felt herself growing warmer — glowing with strange emotions which were flooding through her, making her vividly aware of her own sexual instincts.

He leaned forward and kissed the hollow between her breasts. She looked down at his dark, glossy head and craved to hold it against her bosom.

'Erika said I was a lucky guy,' he said in a firmly controlled voice and Angela experienced a shiver of resentment run through her. Erika, it was always Erika, she thought.

Robert mistook her shiver for a reckless shudder of ecstasy and would have indulged in more intimate exploration, but Angela, fearing her own passion and irritated by the mention of Erika, pushed him away. She tried to cover up her legs but Robert was not so easily dissuaded. He kept his hand in place under her gown.

'I thought we were trying to look at these brochures,' she said in a weak voice.

'You can — I can do two things at once, though one rather better than the other, and I know it pleases you.'

'No, Robert,' she protested, but it was a half-hearted denial. She pulled away from his grasp and stood up, but he grabbed her again and forced her back to sit on his knee.

'The brochures,' he said meaningfully, but first he lifted her left arm and placed it around the back of his neck. She ought to throw him out. She should be livid with him, but how could she be when she loved him so desperately? She was willing to sell her soul for him. She wanted him to do all and more than he did. She needed full satisfaction, but Robert was only playing with her emotions. A woman like Erika would respond more readily, and for a fleeting moment, as Robert read the details of the various tours, Angela's imagination ran riot. If it were Erika here they would make love, shower together, and make love again. They would go to dinner, drink, chat and Erika would be the perfect companion, but every touch, every word would be paving the way for a night of thrills.

Robert seemed to be unaware of her frustration as he took out a pen and ticked the different tours. How quickly his passion subsided, but that she supposed was because he was only playing a game with her.

Eventually he left her to book the sight-seeing tours decided upon for the next two days. Angela closed the door, finished drying her hair, and when Robert returned a good half-hour later she was dressed and applying her make-up. She could hear him moving about, and when his door opened she expected to hear the bathroom door close a second later. Instead he walked into her room again and when she looked up she almost gasped with surprise. At first she thought he was entirely naked. Then she noticed the brief Y-fronts. He was carrying a large sponge-bag, but walked up to her at the dressing-table and returned the brochure and some tickets.

'I'll leave these with you,' he said. 'Look after your tickets. It's all very simple, they pick you up and drop you back here at the hotel.'

'I should have given you some money,' she said, trying not to show her admiration of his bronze, Herculean body. There was a curly thatch of hair, wide on his chest, narrowing towards his slim hips, but it enhanced the shiny, dark brown tan beneath which his powerful muscles rippled with virility. She had never seen a man so superbly masculine, so handsome in every detail. It both delighted and frightened her.

He went to the door. 'You do not have to give me money, Angela. You are here for my benefit — and pleasure,' he tossed over his shoulder as he went out.

He didn't bother shutting the door and, out of the corner of her eye she stole a glimpse as, whistling happily, he returned to his room a few minutes later, hair still dripping from the shower. His burnt-almond body was completely naked now, the extent of his discarded briefs revealed by the contrast of white skin in that area, with the intimate sheath of dark fleece in front. Her feckless admiration took her down forbidden avenues, wondering how he would react to her exploration of his masculinity . . .

When she saw him next her admiration did not lessen in the slightest. He was freshly shaved, hair neatly combed, his body clothed in a dark grey suit with pink shirt and patterned tie. His black slip-on shoes were immaculately polished so that he looked elegantly perfect in every detail.

They went downstairs to dinner.

Angela enjoyed every moment. Although Robert was

much sought-after he was very attentive to her, sitting beside her, his arm round her shoulder. But when she leaned forward, he lowered his arm, drew her closer to him, and began to caress her breast, much to her discomfort. She was sure other people must notice, and his boldness embarrassed her. When they returned to their rooms long after midnight she confronted him.

'Robert, you might be a little more discreet in public. I'm not here just for you to keep mauling me,' she said.

'*Liebling*,' he said kissing her gently, 'my colleagues would think me most unfeeling if I did not pay homage to your lovely figure. I think you English are naïve, and afraid of being too demonstrative. Besides only you and I know the rhapsody we were composing. Sweet dreams Angela.' He kissed her again and went to his own room, closing the door firmly.

* * *

Vienna was oppressively hot despite the season. But it was a glittering city of romance. The first excursion Robert had arranged for her took her on an extensive tour through the city, stopping off at the magnificent Castle of Schöbrunn, once the summer residence of the proud Habsburgs. Her party was escorted through many rooms displaying the Baroque riches of the Habsburg Empire. Having seen the Opera House, State Museums, University, City Hall and Parliament buildings, with a final visit to the grand Belvedere Palace of Prince Eugene of Savoy, Angela was glad of a rest, though the beds at the hotel were excessively hard. After dinner, she talked with some of the wives she had met the previous day. Robert was engrossed in conversation with a small middle-aged man with a neatly clipped beard. He wore gold-rimmed spectacles and beside Robert looked quite dwarf-like. Their business seemed to be very private, and Angela missed Robert's attentiveness.

The next morning she went shopping with some of her new friends and in the afternoon took a coach tour through the Vienna Woods, to the hunting lodge at Mayerling where that tragic couple Prince Rudolph and his mistress had committed suicide in the winter of 1889.

Angela missed Robert's company, and at dinner that evening he seemed subdued, at least until the speeches were made and he was acclaimed as the new chairman. Angela decided that he must have been nervous, though when he made his own speech he showed no lack of confidence.

It was late when they returned to their rooms and Robert only kissed Angela's cheek.

'Congratulations, Robert,' she said, gazing up at him with undisguised longing. 'I think you'll be a worthy chairman.'

'Thank you, Angela. I hope so, though it will mean more work for you and me.' He turned and opened his bedroom door. 'By the way, about lunch tomorrow.'

'Aren't we going home tomorrow?' she asked in surprise, since the conference had now ended.

'No,' Robert said. 'While we are here you must make the most of the opportunity, for if you were in Vienna for a month you would still find something new. I'm afraid we shall have to leave the Opera until another time, but I have booked to take you on a trip to the Hungarian border tomorrow afternoon, and on Sunday morning we shall visit the Spanish Riding Academy.'

'It's very kind of you to go to so much trouble, Robert, but I thought you'd be anxious to get home to the farm,' Angela said honestly.

He ran a finger beneath her chin. 'This is a little holiday for me too,' he said. 'We may as well stay as the weather is so good. Usually it rains when I come to Vienna.'

'What were you going to say about lunch tomorrow?'

'Ah, yes — I have to meet someone. Will you mind eating alone for once?'

'Of course not.'

'I must apologise, *meine lieb*, but it is rather important.'

He disappeared into his bedroom. Angela felt confused by his manner. He seemed either worried or guilty — perhaps both!

She spent another restless night wishing that the Austrians had softer beds. It was hot, too, so she stripped off her cotton nightie, took off the quilt cover and used it as a double sheet to cover her as she lay on top of the feather-filled quilt. Cooler and more comfortable, at last she slept.

A sudden shaft of sunlight woke her to find Robert, wearing only a pair of light brown slacks, drawing back the curtains.

'Are you awake, Angela?' he asked softly.

She yawned and stretched a long bare arm above her head.

'What was the matter?' he continued with concern. 'I heard you moving about in the night.'

Angela grunted sleepily. 'You Austrians must be made of iron,' she mumbled. 'The bed is so hard. I couldn't sleep so I decided to use the duvet as a mattress.'

'Evidently more comfortable,' Robert observed with some amusement, 'even to airing your feet.' He pulled at her bare toes which were sticking out at the foot of the bed, and she realised with dismay that she was entirely naked.

'Come on,' he urged. 'It's time to get up.'

'I can't,' she said. 'Not while you're here.'

His expression changed, and a look of wickedness flashed in his eyes. It was a soul-destroying look and she knew that she could forgive him anything when he looked at her in that demoralising, seductive way. She thought he meant to pull back the cover in order to see for himself the extent of her nakedness. Instead he picked up the lower corner to look, chuckled mischievously and continued to wave it up and down sending a cold draught over her body.

'Robert!' she admonished, drawing her feet up. He made a grab for them, tickling the soles until she was hysterical and the quilt cover was somehow dislodged.

Then he was lying beside her holding her in the warmth of his arms.

'You should have come to me if you couldn't sleep,' he murmured. 'You should be used to hard beds by now, they're much better for you. That's the reason I'm always up at the crack of dawn — but if I had you beside me — mm . . . ' his mouth covered her lips and when she gasped his tongue quickly slid inside to flirt with hers. It drove her insensible. He was a madman, a maniac, and yet as she felt his powerful body pressed to hers she would have needed little persuasion to yield.

But serious lovemaking wasn't in Robert's mind. As Angela looked up with diffident eyes she saw a man who was starved of female company. He needed to flirt and tease and satisfy the exhibitionist in him. And yet as she met his gaze she experienced again that wonderful feeling of complete understanding. For just a second their minds were as one. Like Lilli and Rudolph, Angela remembered.

'Now tell me that I'm an uncivilised brute,' he invited.

His large hand was resting on her hip but not in a sensuous way. She knew that her cheeks were crimson, but what was the point in trying to cover up now? It might evoke another scrabble, and there was no knowing how it might end.

'What do you expect me to say?' she asked huskily.

'At least you have the grace to blush, and so you should, *meine lieb*, you are a *provocateur*.'

'Let me remind you,' she said pointedly, 'that I was sleeping peacefully until you rudely intruded into my privacy.'

'Oh yes,' Robert taunted, 'the privacy you women value so much when all you want really is to be touched. The sense of touch, Angela, is the most important of all.' His gaze was one of devouring curiosity, and while not a finger moved her body felt as if he was caressing every part intimately. It seemed to Angela that all she needed to feel was spiritual possession.

He took a last lingering, covetous look, his eyes finally levelling with hers.

'I've had my shower,' he said quietly. 'Go when you're ready.'

The door closed noiselessly behind him and Angela breathed deeply. She felt as if she'd been starved of oxygen. She ran her fingers lightly across her abdomen, feeling the warmth which his hand had left. She had no doubts about her love for her Herculean baron, but did he love her? There were brief spasmodic moments when she believed he knew how she felt, but Erika had confirmed what Angela had guessed, that Robert used women for revenge. This morning, though, there had been no sign of revenge, only playfulness. She ought to be thankful, for if revenge was what he wanted he would take it with barbaric sadism.

When she was ready to go down for breakfast she knocked on his door. He came out carrying a newspaper rolled up and switched it across her bottom as he opened the main door. He was right, she thought, the sense of touch could bring such a thrill. She didn't care how he touched her as long as he made such gestures.

After breakfast he took her by car to see St Stephen's Cathedral still being restored after war damage, and then to a café.

By his increasingly sombre mood, Angela guessed he was thinking about his luncheon appointment, presumably some business affair that he did not like.

Before leaving her at the hotel, he said, 'Angela, our

tour leaves at two-thirty. I'll meet you in reception.'

When he had gone she walked to the nearby shops to buy small gifts for her grandmother and the family as well as Frau Kiegerl. On her way back to the hotel, she noticed Robert on the other side of the street. He was talking to Erika!

Angela dodged back into the arcade of a jeweller's shop to watch. They were deep in conversation when, a few moments later, the small, bearded man Angela had noticed at the conference joined them and they all moved on inside a nearby restaurant.

All Angela's happiness drained away from her. Had Erika been here at the hotel all the time? Was Angela just being used as a cover-up? While she was enjoying the tours Robert had so conveniently booked for her was Robert somewhere with Erika? She felt sick with misery, and instead of going to have lunch she went to her room and lay down feeling miserably sorry for herself.

She intended to confront Robert with what she had seen, but she had a long wait until two-thirty and in that time she calmed down and thought things out rationally. What was he doing that was wrong? He was a bachelor and had every right to see whom he chose — go to bed with whom he chose for that matter. Angela realised that the reason for her distress was jealousy. Robert could be jolly with her, but it never progressed beyond horseplay. His kisses were flippant and she was a fool to read more into them. He kept his virility for Erika — the lovely Erika — and the reason they weren't married was Frau Kiegerl's dislike of her.

With fifteen minutes still to go she got ready and took a magazine with her to reception. She sat by a large rubber plant where she hoped no one would notice her.

People began to assemble and the coach drew up outside, but there was no sign of Robert. Had he left her stranded? She couldn't get on the coach with the others as she had no ticket. Perhaps he'd never even booked!

The engine of the coach sprang to life. Then she heard raised voices — who else but Robert, she thought — and folded up her magazine. He was offering the tickets to the courier, and looking through the windows of the coach. When the courier spotted Angela casually walking across the pavement he spoke to Robert, who wheeled round on her.

'Why didn't you get your seat, darling?' he asked.

Darling indeed, Angela thought piously, but Robert wasn't angry, only concerned.

'I couldn't get on without a ticket,' she said.

'I'd told Karl to expect you,' Robert explained, helping her up.

'And I saved the best seats for you,' the courier said getting in behind Robert.

As soon as they were settled Robert took her hand, intertwining her fingers with his. He was elated — well of course he was, she thought, hadn't he just been with Erika?

'Have a good lunch?' he whispered, snugly fitting his massive frame closer to hers.

Oh, what was the use, she thought, she simply couldn't keep up the pretence of being indifferent.

'Lovely, thanks,' she answered, smiling up at him. 'How was yours?'

8

Robert pursed his lips. 'It was a necessary meeting,' he said solemnly. 'I'm sorry if I kept you waiting.'

Angela turned her head to look at the passing scenery. She must resign herself to making the best of things. At least Robert was here with her now even if he was wishing that it was Erika who sat beside him. He seemed bent on enjoying himself and gave Angela all his attention.

After visiting the palace of Esterhazy, where Haydn had worked as a musician for many years, they stopped for light refreshments. Angela, having missed lunch, was profoundly grateful. They visited the inevitable gift shop at the Roman quarry of S. Margarethen and stopped in the famous village of Rust, with its numerous patrician houses dating back to the Renaissance.

Everyone took pictures of the storks surveying the world from their huge nests on the chimneys.

After a look at the grim Hungarian look-out posts on the border, they drove back to Lake Neusiedl and boarded a boat to cross the lake, hoping to spot some of the rare birds which find a refuge in its reed beds. On the other side, the whole party boarded a large, horse-drawn cart with rows of wooden benches seating twenty people. The elderly driver produced a two-litre bottle of local wine and as was the custom, passed it round until the bottle was empty.

The cart took them to a restaurant, where a waitress in Hungarian gipsy costume served them with extra-tall tumblers filled with more of the local white wine.

'Only sip it, Angela, or you will soon be drunk,' Robert

warned. 'I won't mind, of course,' he added with a huge grin, 'but I think you would be unhappy afterwards.'

He led her into the garden. Wooden picnic tables and benches were set out surrounding a circular brick barbecue fire, where they toasted cubes of bread and bacon fat.

'You must eat plenty of this to keep you sober,' Karl told them.

When it began to get dark, they went into the restaurant, where yet more wine was served with the meal and they were serenaded by gipsy musicians in the candlelight.

'Are you enjoying it?' Robert whispered, his arm around Angela as she sipped coffee to try to keep her head steady.

'It's been wonderful, Robert,' she breathed. He kissed her cheek and a camera flashed, as if they had set it off. Robert laughed, grasped Angela's hand, and took her out to the floor where others were already dancing. He pulled her close, gazing lovingly into her eyes and holding her small hand tightly in his own. She thought her heart would burst with love for him.

Karl, the courier, eventually persuaded his party to board the bus once more, and all too soon the bright lights of Vienna drew closer.

'There is more, so much more that I would like to show you,' Robert said as they sat huddled together in the front seat of the coach.

'It's been wonderful,' Angela enthused, still a little dizzy from the effects of the wine. 'A lovely way to end my holiday.'

'There's next summer, if you're still here,' Robert replied. 'Have you been to the Prater?'

'No,' Angela said, 'but I've seen pictures of the huge ferris wheel.'

'You get a lovely view of Vienna from it, but you will do

well to leave that until next spring or summer.'

Next spring or summer. Where would Angela be then? It was obvious that Robert thought she would have returned to England . . .

She would have to think seriously about her future plans. One part of her longed to be home with her father but the other side of her nature was searching for something indefinable which she had imagined lay here in the country of her mother's origin.

Today she had found that something. Just being with Robert, and knowing that whatever feelings he had for her, she loved everything about him. The good, the kind, as well as the bad. Without thinking she placed her hand on his thigh, gently caressing, remembering with admiration the sight of him without clothes, her bronze Herculean master.

Robert stretched out his long legs in front of him and gave a small significant groan. Immediately Angela retracted. What was she thinking of? It must be the wine causing her to be so reckless and she felt her cheeks turning crimson. Robert chuckled and replaced her hand on his leg, covering it with his own.

Karl had worked his way to the front of the coach.

'Your hotel is the last port of call,' he said to Robert, 'but some of the others are keen to stop off at a night club in Vienna.'

Robert looked at Angela. One look was enough, a look which told him that she was as eager as he to get back to the hotel although it was barely ten o'clock.

'We have to go home tomorrow,' Robert explained to Karl. 'We still have a few things to do in the morning, so I think we must say no.' His thumb kept up a gentle rhythm on the back of Angela's hand.

Angela wanted to reach the hotel, yet some inner voice was warning her that once they moved, the lovely feeling of togetherness they were sharing would be lost. But they were closer at this moment than ever before, and nothing could take away such profound happiness.

Finally they said goodbye to Karl, and within minutes Robert was fitting the key into the lock of Angela's door. He followed her in.

'Robert,' Angela said coyly, 'that was the best trip of all — because you were with me to enjoy it too.'

With his magnetic gaze fixed on her, Angela clasped her arms about his neck and pulled his head down to kiss him. They were hungry for each other, Angela shamelessly arousing him as she refused to release his lips. They laughed childishly as they started to remove each other's clothes.

Angela thought the bell she heard was some sort of alarm. Robert, removing her blouse to kiss her bare shoulder, paused to listen.

'Telephone,' he whispered, 'in my room.'

He swung away from her, picked up his jacket and tie and went out of the room, calling over his shoulder: 'Goodnight, Angela. Sleep well. Breakfast at eight o'clock.'

Although he pulled the door behind him, his loud voice came clearly through the wall. 'Erika! — you timed that well. Where are you?'

Angela couldn't bear to listen to any more, and anyway Robert quickly lowered his voice.

No wonder he didn't want to go on to a night club. His anxiety to return to the hotel wasn't caused by his desire for Angela. He was expecting a call from Erika!

Angela looked down at herself. She was half undressed. All she had managed to do was undo a couple of Robert's shirt buttons, but she had slid her hands inside and for the first time lovingly explored his body. Surely he must know how crazy with love for him she was? But he didn't care, he was only whiling away the time with her, waiting for the telephone to ring.

Angela was certain that it had all been arranged. She felt too unhappy to cry, realising what a fool she had made of herself. As she prepared for bed, conscious of Robert's low, seductive voice in the next room, she grew bitter. Why had he even bothered to go on the afternoon trip if he was expecting to hear from Erika again?

* * *

Angela didn't know how she sat through breakfast next morning, or how she managed to show her appreciation of the visit to the Spanish Riding School. She had only one thought in her mind and that was to start back for Deutschlandsberg. When they did she sat mute, letting Robert concentrate on his driving while she tried to decide what to do.

Should she leave the hall at once, or should she wait until the next letter came from England, and then tell Robert she was too homesick to stay?

She was too proud to confess her love for him, knowing that he had no one but Erika on his mind. She could not, dare not, give way to her feelings or Robert would recognise her jealousy at once, but her heart was heavy. She couldn't imagine how she was to continue living and working at the hall.

But such was Frau Kiegerl's delight at having them home again that the days passed by rapidly without Angela coming to any conclusions. She kept reminding herself that if she stayed she would only suffer more heartache, yet she simply couldn't bring herself to make the arrangements to go home.

She was a coward. Robert would sneer and pride himself on forecasting her behaviour correctly.

Everything on the farm was being prepared for winter now, and Angela found that there was more work for her to do. Robert spent more time in the office working with her, another reason for not returning to England. As long as there was no mention of Erika, the disappointments of Vienna faded. She got to know him even better, understood his irritability when things went wrong due to someone's carelessness.

She loved him the more for his devotion to his mother, and for the natural way he accepted her. There were no more suggestions about keeping him happy in bed, and she realised now that in his strange way he had been trying her out. Once she responded he had put her firmly back in the slot he had employed her to occupy.

Sometimes he would visit Graz, but Angela never heard whether he visited Lotte or Erika.

It grew increasingly cold. First the frosts came and then the heavy falls of snow. One day, when the postman trudged into the office shivering, Angela made him some hot soup in the kitchen.

On her return Robert was opening the post. He paused to toss her a couple of bills, then he came to an airmail letter which he handed to her with a gentle smile.

'England was never like this, Angela?' he said watching her reaction carefully.

'Only on rare occasions.'

'One winter here and you'll be glad to go home,' he said.

When Robert went out with the postman, she opened her father's letter. He started off in the usual way, then went on to say how lonely his life had become with Angela settled in Austria and Nick and Tim both married. He loved his family, he said, and he had kept going on the happy memories of family life over the past thirty-odd years, but his loneliness was now too great to bear alone.

The shock came on the final page. He was about to marry again.

Angela went cold. She could hardly believe it. She read and re-read the letter, unaware that Robert had returned and was standing in front of her desk observing her.

'Angela?' It was the concern in his voice which brought her back to the time and place. 'Not bad news I hope?'

She crumpled the letter up in her hand and let it drop at the side of the typewriter. Then she buried her face in her hands. No, she would not let Robert see her cry, but the lump in her throat clogged her voice, and in spite of all her brave resolutions the tears pricked, materialising wilfully until she was blinded, her chin trembling convulsively.

She was vaguely aware of Robert striding about, and then his arm was round her, and for a few seconds she allowed the tears to escape freely. Angela tried to get up. She wanted to escape, run to her room and weep alone.

'Angela, *liebling*. Tell me? Share your grief with me, *bitte*?'

Grief? What was Robert talking about? She ought not to be grieving, but singing with joy. She dried her eyes, averting them from Robert and then gave a nervous laugh.

'I don't know why I'm crying,' she said huskily. 'I should be laughing. My father,' she gulped, 'he's getting married again.'

Robert's hand smoothed her back comfortingly. 'This was a surprise?' he asked gently. 'Your father did not mention anything before?'

'Nothing,' Angela said. 'I had no idea.'

'You think perhaps he is being disloyal to the memory of your mother,' Robert said as if voicing his own opinion.

'It can't have been easy for him,' Angela said. She read the letter again, this time more slowly, listening in her mind for her father's familiar voice framing the words from the pages of his letter.

The more she thought about her father the more guilty she felt. She had been so selfish, thinking only of her own happiness in wanting to stay with her mother's family, allowing him to go home to that desolate house alone.

How could she have been so insensitive? How grieved her mother would be to know that Angela had cared so little.

Her first instinct was to pack her case and leave at once, but she soon realised that all her good intentions came far too late. Her father had found someone else, and the last thing he would want was Angela turning up to interfere. She suddenly felt empty inside, realising that home in England wouldn't be her home any more. She'd come to think of home as here at the hall, but over lunch as she glanced from Robert to his mother she felt like a stranger again.

'You must telephone your family, Angela,' Robert suggested later.

'Dad says in his letter that he has written to Grandma already.'

'But you would like to discuss it with them — yes?' he went on.

'I shall see them the day after tomorrow.'

'You must telephone your father then — this evening.'

There were times when Angela objected to Robert's dominance, and for a second she felt like telling him to mind his own business, but by evening she had recovered a little from the shock and was able to speak to her father without showing too much emotion.

She returned to the little sitting room where Frau Kiegerl was reading. The old lady looked up smiling in response to Angela's radiant face.

'I spoke to her,' Angela said eagerly. 'Her name is Laura and she sounds very nice. They aren't going to be married until the spring, but she lives a few streets away so goes every day to look after Dad.'

'You'll be wanting to go home now?' Frau Kiegerl asked.

'For the wedding. They're each going to sell their own houses and buy a bungalow somewhere on the edge of town.'

She was going to add that Laura and her father had both assured her of a permanent home with them if she ever needed it, but the lump was back in her throat and she knew what loneliness really meant — the empty feeling that she didn't belong to anyone. Where would she go when Robert didn't need her any more?

Angela went to bed that night with confused hopes and fears milling inside her, not really knowing where her own future lay. She was pleased for her father, and during the next few days felt more content when she heard from her brothers that Laura was a kindly widow who was looking for companionship.

But still her feeling of being unwanted remained. Her love for Robert had grown into something deep, something so much more lasting than a sexual relationship. She knew she was going to be hurt. Robert was kind most of the time, but he seldom made any of the flirtatious gestures she had found so appealing. It was as if he had erected a barrier between them since the conference in Vienna, instructing Angela to remain strictly on the side of the secretary while he remained very much her boss.

Angela's one consolation was that Erika was unlikely to visit the hall. She remembered with embarrassment the only time Frau Kiegerl had mentioned Erika to her, and that was soon after their return from Vienna, when Angela had mentioned Erika's phone call.

Frau Kiegerl had suddenly leaned forward in her chair and asked in a suppressed voice: 'Was that woman there?'

'Oh no,' Angela lied, 'I didn't see anyone I knew at the conference.'

She had wanted to save Robert's mother from the aggravation which the knowledge of secret meetings between Robert and Erika would cause.

There were more frequent letters from England as the weeks drew nearer to Christmas. Already Robert and Frau Kiegerl were speculating on Angela's return in the spring, assuming that when she went she would not be returning to Austria, but Angela was making no plans. At every mention of England she remembered that her father would have Laura, that Christopher had his wife — and that she would have no one.

She began to be obsessed with the feeling that she was alone in the world, and when Andreas telephoned one day and said he would be in Deutschlandsberg she agreed to spend an evening with him.

She announced at lunch that she was going out to dinner with Andreas, but it was received with stony silence. She couldn't think why, nor did she greatly care. Andreas was fun to be with and he made her laugh, so that she returned to the hall with sparkling eyes and her lips refreshed by his tender kisses.

Well, she thought as she crept up the stairs, wasn't Andreas better than no one?

After that, Andreas would often telephone and they would laugh and chat. When he rang during working hours Robert made a point of leaving the office. Clearly, Angela's friendship with Andreas displeased him.

During a mild spell, Josef took the opportunity to drive into Graz to see Lotte, and he invited Angela to accompany him. Andreas met her and took her to a luxurious hotel for lunch. Then, to her surprise, he went to the reception desk and asked for a key.

Angela, puzzled, made no comment. They went by lift to a room on one of the upper floors, where Andreas removed his jacket and tie.

'My flat's not very convenient,' he explained. 'It's only one room over the surgery, in fact, and whoever is on call expects to share my heat, and television and any food available.'

He closed the venetian blinds, turned down the bed covers, and switched the radio on to some pleasant music. Then he held her against him hard and kissed her. Before she could stop him he was helping her to undress, but although he was gently persuasive there was little passion in his efforts, while Angela was seeing Robert, the bronze Hercules, instead of Andreas beside her. She remained passive, and for a few moments felt as if she were looking down at herself, a slim youthful girl of twenty-one with white skin, a well-developed bust, neat waist and nicely moulded hips. Her dark hair was splayed out over the pillow and a stranger's fingers were entwined among the tresses. His soft moist lips explored her body, but occasionally he paused to search her glazed expression. His hands slid sensuously over her shoulders and she shivered. She felt cold and recalled Christopher telling her that she was never more than lukewarm.

Of course she was lukewarm with Christopher — or Andreas. Only one man could arouse her to a state of feverish excitement . . .

Andreas was not caressing her any more, but gazing placidly into her face. 'Angela?' he whispered.

She shook her head. 'I didn't come here for this, Andreas,' she whispered miserably. 'I'm sorry if I misled you.'

'I thought the modern English girl could only be satisfied in bed,' he said with an excusing grin.

'Then you know now it isn't true,' she replied calmly.

The thought crossed her mind that she had foolishly exposed herself to all kinds of misuse. It was this sort of situation which sometimes led a man to brutality, even murder, she supposed, but she knew that she was safe enough with Andreas. He went limp beside her, one arm thrown carelessly across her waist, and in a few moments he was breathing deeply in sleep.

Angela pulled the covers up over them. She lay still, thankful that Andreas was not the passionate lover he pretended to be. Evidently he didn't find her attractive enough, and had arranged all this believing it was what she wanted. Did she appear so promiscuous? What was it Robert had called her? A *provocateur*. If only he would realise that her provocation — love — was only directed at him. She had been stupid to imagine that a friendship with Andreas would help to fill the aching void in her heart. Nothing could ever fill the space she had reserved for Robert. But he had Erika, so it was stalemate.

She slipped out of bed and dressed, hoping she would be able to find her way back to the park where they had arranged to meet Josef. She was zipping up her fleece-lined boots when Andreas rolled on to his back, rubbed his eyes and sat up.

'Where are you going?' he asked sleepily.

Angela shrugged. 'There's no point in staying here,' she said.

'Forgive me, Angela. I have treated you badly. What must think of me going to sleep instead of — ?'

'There's no need to pretend, Andreas.' She looked away embarrassed. 'Can't we just be friends?'

He looked at her and smiled, and she guessed that in some way he was lonely too, but grateful for her candour.

'I hope we will always be that, Angela, but I think for you there is someone, somewhere, for whom you are saving yourself. I admire you for this.'

'And you?' she asked hesitantly. 'I think we have mutual respect for each other, but let's be honest, we simply don't love each other. You didn't really want to make love to me.'

Andreas swivelled round on the bed and put his long legs over the side. Angela turned away while he dressed thinking how completely different he was from Robert. Andreas was pale-skinned, leaner than Robert and with little of his aggressive maleness and rugged strength.

'Any man would wish to make love to you, Angela, *meine lieb*, but I have never forced my attentions on a woman yet and I hope I never shall. There is no harm done, there are many days ahead when we can learn to love each other, perhaps.'

When they emerged into the street again he pulled Angela's hand through his arm and they walked along happily on the way to meet Lotte and Josef.

'Was Lotte the girl Robert loved in England?' Angela asked.

Andreas laughed. 'No one will ever know which woman Robert loves,' he said. 'Perhaps he loves them all, and certainly they all love him.'

He squeezed her hand significantly. Andreas was no fool. She guessed that she had given her secret away.

On the drive back to Deutschlandsberg, Angela and Josef didn't talk much as both were occupied with their own thoughts. Josef asked Angela if she had enjoyed her day with Andreas. She had noticed a slight edge to her cousin's voice and wondered whether Josef had the same idea about modern English girls as Andreas.

'We had a lovely meal,' she told him, 'but after that I think I disappointed him. He seems to think English girls are only interested in going to bed. Now I think we have a better arrangement — we're just good friends.'

Josef remained silent for several seconds, keeping his head erect and looking directly in front of him.

'That is all Andreas should be,' he said levelly. 'He is a married man with two children.'

9

Angela was too paralysed to speak. She'd been an even bigger fool than she realised. Now she understood Andreas's reluctance, but what a stupid man he was to book a hotel room simply because of the rogue reputation of English girls!

'I didn't know,' she said softly. 'He never said, which was very wrong of him. He has no right even to take me out.'

'They are separated, but I think they will not remain so much longer. Andreas is away from home so much that it has not been easy for his wife, but I think he will soon miss the comforts of home and return to his wife and children.'

'I wish I'd known, perhaps I could have persuaded him to go back.'

'Then you are not in love with him?' Josef asked.

'No, did you really think I was?' she asked in surprise.

'Yes, we were all afraid that your low spirits were due to being fond of Andreas and knowing that he was a married man. I'm so relieved, Angela.'

'I'm glad you've told me. He's a nice man and we've spent a pleasant afternoon window shopping and looking round Graz. But that's all!'

She didn't dare imagine how different the situation might have been if she had been willing to let Andreas . . . But it hadn't happened. Perhaps Andreas had simply used her to prove his freedom. A freedom he didn't really want.

'I've been rather naïve,' she went on. 'Frau Kiegerl and

Robert went very quiet when I said I was meeting Andreas. I realise now they must have disapproved. But how was your day, Josef?'

'Excellent,' he said enthusiastically.

'Is this really serious, Josef?' Angela pursued. 'Isn't Lotte dedicated to her profession?'

'Oh yes, of course, but that does not mean she doesn't want to get married and have children. Let us not get weighed down with the problems just yet. We are in love and very happy. I hope you are happy for us, Angela?'

'I am indeed — but a little sorry for Robert if Lotte is the woman he loves.'

'Lotte? Robert? Whatever gave you that idea, Angela?'

She went on to tell Josef what Andreas had told her at the party.

'Lotte and Robert were in England at the same time years ago, but for Lotte it was a good friendship, nothing more. I can't speak for Robert. He is devoted to his mother and his estate. He has many women. He is a very popular man and few women wouldn't be attracted by his position, but he keeps them all guessing.'

Angela looked out of the window at the low grey clouds and saw a new cascade of snowflakes falling on an already white landscape. Here was one woman for whom status meant nothing. She would settle for Robert's love.

By the time they reached the hall, snow was falling heavily. Angela said goodbye to Josef and let herself in through the solid front door. She stamped her feet on the doormat and shook her sheepskin coat, which was splattered with white dots of cottonwool even though she had run the few yards from the car.

Robert appeared from the small sitting room. He looked big and bulky, in a thick blue sweater.

'Angela,' he said, greeting her in a more subdued tone than usual. Did she detect a slight hint of rebuke? 'You had an unpleasant journey home?'

'Not too bad,' Angela said. 'It's snowing hard now though. I hope Josef will get back to the farm all right.'

'I'm sure he will. We're used to this weather here. Come and warm yourself with some coffee.'

'I could smell it as soon as I opened the door. It's heavenly.' She looked up into his cool eyes wishing she had the courage to say that the sight of him was more warming than the coffee. But his expression was not cordial.

He allowed her to go first into the sitting room, where a log fire burned cheerily in the fireplace. She rubbed her hands at the fire.

'Not too close,' Robert warned her. 'You'll get chilblains.'

'Where's your mother?' Angela asked.

'Gone to bed. It's after eleven.'

Angela looked at the clock in disbelief. 'Is it that time? I suppose the weather slowed us up more than I'd realised.'

He handed her a cup of coffee and she looked up under heavy lids. She wanted him to be kind, to show some sign of pleasantness which would reward her for the love she felt for him. But his expression was hard.

'You seem annoyed, Robert. Does it worry you that Josef and Lotte have become friends — are in love?' she added.

'I am delighted for them, but I am disappointed in you, Angela. I thought you had high moral principles. Where have you been all day? What have you and Andreas Klug been up to?'

His suspicions made her suddenly angry. 'What's the matter with you men for heaven's sake?' she almost shouted, her eyes blazing. 'Don't you have such a thing in this part of the world as good old-fashioned friendship? It's no thanks to you that I haven't been up to anything with Andreas. You seem to have forgotten to introduce him to me as a married man with children. Not that I wanted that kind of relationship with him anyway. He's been very kind and is good company, fun to be with, but when I love someone, Robert, I'm faithful, no matter what!'

She turned her back on him and gazed into the fire through a mist of emotion. Another minute and she would have declared her love for him, but that was her secret. She must never become so incensed that she carelessly revealed the desires of her stubborn heart. She'd never be able to stand his mockery.

'I thought you knew that Andreas was married,' Robert said with surprise. 'Surely Josef told you.'

She turned on him again. 'Well he didn't. You aren't very good at communicating, Robert, but if you're so concerned for my welfare here's the truth for what it's worth. I had lunch at a hotel with Andreas, and then he took me to one of the hotel bedrooms.' The horrified look on Robert's face goading her into shocking him even more. 'Despicable, isn't it?' she taunted. 'Going to a hotel bedroom with a married man! Only *I* didn't know he was married!'

Robert took a long stride forward. Angela backed away, fearful for one awful moment that he was going to strike her.

'You mean you'd have — ? If he hadn't been married?'

Angela felt that she'd suddenly gained some power over Robert.

'I didn't know he was married *until we were on our way home.*' She had scored. The expression on Robert's face was a mixture of disbelief and anger. She didn't intend to divulge any more. What business was it of his whether Andreas and she had made love or not? He evidently chose to think the worst of them. She finished her coffee and left the room without wishing him goodnight.

She felt sick inside. Sick that she had unwittingly caused so much worry to her relations as well as Robert and his mother, not to mention the shock of having found herself in such a situation. At least she had ended the day by being honest with Andreas. He hadn't been with her, but perhaps he had thought she knew he was married.

And now she had been less than honest with Robert. Despite her defence of integrity she had let him think that she and Andreas had been lovers. That was his fault, she thought, if he chose to indulge in such illusions.

But perhaps his illusions were not so unreasonable. She had responded passionately to his love-making so it was only natural that he would expect her to behave similarly with Andreas. What Robert did not know was that Angela loved her bronze Hercules too much to allow any other man the privilege of knowing her intimately.

Frau Kiegerl was somewhat distant with Angela for the next two or three days, but as the snow deepened and they were forced more into each other's company they became closer than before.

There were preparations to be made for Christmas and when Robert went into the town, Angela went with him to do some Christmas shopping.

'So you're not leaving us just yet then?' Robert said, for once without a sneer as he helped her with her parcels.

'I shall go home in the spring for the wedding,' she replied. 'But when you have had enough of me you have only to say and I can go back to the farm in Deutschlandsberg.'

'For that,' he said with a wicked grin, 'you can walk home.'

Gradually over the past few days she had watched his censoriousness decrease. She knew he was teasing her now, so she tossed her head haughtily and started walking. He overtook her and pulled to a halt. She walked straight on past him, head in the air. He overtook her again. She walked on by. She heard him chugging up behind her, slowly, until his bumper was almost touching her. She didn't even turn round and they went some distance like this. Then he revved up and shot past her, screeched to a stop and jumped out of the driving seat. With two long strides he reached her, sweeping her up in his arms and depositing her roughly in the back of the vehicle on a heap of sacks. He drove like a madman so that she rolled from side to side, quite unable to sit up until they stopped at a junction.

Robert laughed over his shoulder. 'Come on then, back in your seat,' he called condescendingly and waited until she was by his side.

'I'll be covered with bruises,' she complained, but good-naturedly.

On the morning of Christmas Eve there were a string of visitors to the hall. Angela looked up in surprise when she heard Andreas's voice. A moment later he came into the office.

'So you're going to your relations for Christmas,' Andreas said, 'and then I hear you're going to learn to ski?'

'I don't know about that,' Angela said. 'I mentioned I'd like to, and Josef has said he'd take me up in the Little Alps at the weekends.'

'I wanted to see you alone, Angela, to give you this. It's not much, just a token of affection for you and – ' he looked embarrassed as he fingered the small gaily wrapped box, 'I want to say thank you for being you. I . . . I have been foolish, perhaps not accepting my responsibilities as I should have done. I think you showed me what loyalty really meant. I am happy to say I am going home to my family for Christmas.'

'I'm very pleased, Andreas, and thank you for this, but you shouldn't have. I don't know anything about marriage, but I feel certain it will work if you really want it to.'

'I shall remember always that you said that, and I shall wish for you some happiness too.' He came to the side of her desk and she stood up to receive his kiss. At that moment Robert came in.

Andreas broke off smartly, wished her a happy Christmas, and hurried off to see Robert's mother. Robert said nothing, and followed him out.

Frau Kiegerl insisted that work in the office must finish at mid-day so Angela went to her room and finished packing before Lilli and Rudolph arrived for lunch.

It was the first of the festive meals — laid on especially for Angela because she would not be staying at the hall. She had placed gifts for Robert, his mother and Eva on the Christmas tree which stood majestically in the hall.

It was growing dark when Josef arrived to fetch her. He was invited in for a drink while Angela went to fetch her coat. She was checking that she had everything packed when Robert walked into her room.

'I'll take your case,' he said.

Angela thanked him, thinking he looked a little crestfallen. Her heart warmed to him in sympathy. She supposed he was wishing that Erika could spend Christmas with him. Although he would have all his family round him he would probably be lonely for the woman he loved, just as Angela would be for him.

'Are you sure you have everything?' he asked.

'Quite sure — all that I need,' she said. 'I'm coming back you know!'

His hands reached out and grasped her shoulders: he gazed intently into her face.

'Good,' he said in a gravelly voice. 'Have a happy time, Angela,' he said and kissed her tenderly.

'You too, Robert,' she said bravely, hoping he did not notice the moistness in her eyes or the quiver of her chin. The thought of not seeing him for a whole week was almost unbearable.

He picked up her case and with one hand round her shoulder guided her out on to the landing.

'Christmas, New Year, and before you know it spring will be here. It will not be long before you see your own English family again, Angela.'

She knew he meant to be kind, but it wasn't much compensation.

When she reached Deutschlandsberg there was a heap of mail waiting for her. There were packages too, but Aunt Hilde whisked them away to place under the Christmas tree until tomorrow.

On one, an oblong box, Angela recognised Christopher's handwriting. He was married to someone else. What was he doing sending presents to her?

She opened it and a card fell out with the words, "To my darling sweetheart." A small silver pendant in the shape of a key was wrapped in tissue paper. Hardly able to believe her eyes, Angela read the enclosed letter.

"The Key," Christopher wrote, "is not only to my heart, but also our home, now ready and waiting for your return." He went on to explain that he had only told her he had met someone else in the hope that she would return immediately to England. He was now begging her to do just that, so that they could be married without delay. He enclosed an air ticket for mid-January, along with a photograph of himself standing in front of a newly built bungalow.

Angela opened her mouth but no sound came. She was utterly speechless. Aunt Hilde looked over her shoulder and saw the glittering pendant.

'*Na, na, na!*' she scolded. 'Not until tomorrow.'

Still not really believing Christopher's letter herself, she tried to explain the situation to her aunt.

'You're going home?' her aunt looked amazed.

'I . . . I don't know, Aunt Hilde. He's sent me a ticket. I . . . I must have time to think.'

But inside her the beautiful thought welled up that someone wanted her. Christopher had wanted her all along, and now he was desperate to see her again. She couldn't explain it, but she felt light-headed, as if all her troubles had dissolved like snowflakes falling in a river.

The family rejoiced with her, though she had great difficulty in getting Grandma to believe that she could possibly want to go home. The exuberance lasted all over Christmas Day, but when present-giving time came round Angela's thoughts were steered away from England and Christopher.

The family at the farm had all contributed to buy her a lovely blue ski-suit, and when all the other presents had been opened Josef went out to bring in a brand new pair of skis.

'For you, Angela,' he said, 'with all good wishes from Robert.'

Angela had felt as if someone had stuck a knife into her. How could she have been so carried away by Christopher's promises that she had forgotten the man she really loved?

'Robert couldn't wrap them, Angela,' Josef explained as she stroked the varnished wood, 'so he asked me to hide them until today. Here are some more things from the hall.'

There were sheepskin mittens and a woollen cap to match her ski-suit from Frau Kiegerl, and from Lilli and Rudolph a warm fair-isle jumper. She was overwhelmed with gratitude but, inside her, her heart was crying as the family reminded her that she wouldn't be able to use any of her gifts for long.

'You can always go to Scotland,' Josef said cheerfully.

Deep down, Angela knew she didn't want to go home, that she would never marry Christopher. But how could she retreat now? The airline ticket seemed to make her journey obligatory, so she carried on the deception, at night lying awake defeated and miserable, guilty that she would go home only to tell Christopher that she couldn't go through with it. She was going home in the spring anyway. Now she would simply be going a few weeks earlier?

She dreaded having to tell Robert. But hadn't he remarked that spring would soon be here? Hadn't he said all along that she would return to England?

He would never know the agony of such a journey: the miles that would stretch between them when she would have been content to stay and work for Robert for ever!

She supposed that in time she might come to mean something special to him. But what hope was there when he carried a torch for some other English girl he had known fifteen years ago? And then there was Erika. It was sensible to make the break now however hard it was. Just thinking about it became unbearable.

She kept looking at the airline ticket and the pendant, neither of which gave her any joy at all. In her loneliness she had been vulnerable, and Christopher's offer had seemed to make everything better. He wanted her. But she knew he meant nothing to her now. Marriage to him couldn't possibly work.

The day after Boxing Day Lotte drove in from Graz, and Josef insisted that they take Angela up to the Little Alps for a lesson on her new skis.

They spent a happy afternoon in spite of Angela's trepidation at going high up among the snow-covered mountains in a chair-lift. Her first attempts at ski-ing, accompanied by quite a few tumbles, caused great laughter, but by the end she was beginning to get the hang of it.

Lotte stayed overnight, sharing a room in the now crowded farmhouse with Angela.

When they were both in bed Lotte said, 'Angela you can put out the light, but perhaps you want to talk?'

Something in her voice told Angela that Lotte had noticed the disturbed state of her emotions.

'You are not too sure of things, Angela?' Lotte

whispered from across their bedroom.

'Why do you say that?'

Lotte laughed. 'I am trained to observe, and there is no better way to learn it than with children. Angela, I'm sorry, but I know you are not happy.'

'I hoped it didn't show.'

'Do you want to tell me about it?' Lotte asked kindly. 'I won't repeat anything, not even to Josef, if that is what you wish.'

'It's that . . . I don't really want to go home . . . Well, I do, just to see my father and brothers . . . But everything I want is here.'

'You mean you are going back at this man's command, to marry him, and yet you don't love him?'

'Oh, Lotte – I'm so glad to talk to someone. You must think me so irresponsible. First Andreas – he was kind, showed me attention and I was flattered.'

'We all like to be flattered, Angela,' Lotte said. 'But love is different. When it happens you know that it has happened.'

'I do know – but the man I love doesn't love me, he loves someone else,' Angela said in a croaky voice.

'But if your feelings are genuine, Angela, you cannot marry Christopher, it would not be fair to him.'

'I know, and I don't intend to marry him. I keep trying to write to explain, but it's so difficult. I don't want to hurt him.'

'Even though he hurt you?'

'I don't suppose he meant to . . . '

'But are you going home?'

'I was going anyway, for my father's wedding. Everyone here assumes I'm going on the ticket Christopher sent so they also assume I shall marry him.'

'Well, you said you would. Did you, perhaps, see Christopher's offer as a way to solve your own problems?'

Angela remained silent for a few moments. 'I suppose I

did, but now that I've had time to think about it I know it's not the answer.'

'Perhaps if you make up your mind to go home you will find that everything works out for the best. Why not write and tell Christopher that you were going home anyway, that you're flattered he still wants to marry you, but he must court you again. You must begin at the beginning, Angela. I think it would be wrong to decide too quickly. You may feel quite differently when you get home among your family and friends.'

'Yes, I'll do that,' Angela agreed. 'Thank you, Lotte. I needed someone to talk to.'

'You can always come back here again,' Lotte finished hopefully.

It snowed so heavily the next day that they were confined to the house. Josef and his father had work to do with the animals and Lotte had to return to Graz.

At last Angela managed to write a letter to Christopher — without committing herself to anything. She was sitting with her grandmother watching television when the telephone rang.

'Angela, hurry, it's your father,' Uncle Franz called, and she ran excitedly to the phone.

'I believe you might be coming home sooner that we thought, darling?' he said.

'You've seen Chris then?'

'Yes. He told me he'd written and sent you your fare home.'

'He did, but I haven't really decided yet.'

'Angela, my dear, forgive me, this is so difficult with hundreds of miles between us and perhaps I ought not to ask, but do you love Christopher?'

She wanted to scream 'NO' down the line, but instead, she said, 'I never expected him to come back into my life, Dad. Naturally I'd got over him after all this time, especially believing he was married.'

'Darling, I know I shouldn't tell tales, but I doubt that he's been honest with you. Nick and Tim are ready to tear him limb from limb . . . I suppose he's told you about his new bungalow?'

'Yes, he sent me a picture.'

'Darling — would you really consider stepping into another woman's shoes?'

'What do you mean, Dad? Chris says he only told me he'd got married thinking I'd rush home.'

'He didn't marry her, though they did live together until a couple of weeks ago.'

Angela felt herself go cold with rage. 'Dad, are you sure?'

'I wish I could say no, my dear, but I'm afraid that's the truth. However, in the circumstances perhaps it would be best if you were to come home and get things sorted out.'

'I'm coming home for the wedding,' she said with determination. 'Not before.'

She tried not to show that she was upset when she returned to the living room. But she was angry and humiliated at Christopher's deceit. At least she was certain that she was not going to marry him now.

10

Angela wasn't due back at the hall until January 4th, and after Christmas the days began to drag. Although it was cold she took long walks with the dogs. One afternoon she was playing with them in a field at the back of the farm, throwing snowballs for them to snap at. Suddenly she realised that someone was throwing snowballs at her. She looked round, mystified, and there he was — big and solid in a sheepskin coat with the collar turned up, collecting snow between his bare hands ready to hurl at her.

'Robert!' she exclaimed, and despite the barrage of snow that whizzed through the air towards her she ran to greet him, her green eyes sparkling with more than their usual brightness.

'Robert!' she said again, dodging another snowball, 'what are you doing here?'

'I've come to fetch my secretary,' he said embracing her affectionately.

'Is something wrong?' she asked nervously. The very warmth of him excited her, though she tried to quell such thoughts.

'Yes, I'm afraid so, *meine lieb*. You warned me never to do again what I am about to do, only this time I can give you until ten o'clock tomorrow morning to prepare yourself for a trip to the mountains.'

She looked up in surprise. He was wearing his glasses, and she thought how distinguished the dark rims made him look.

'Lilli and Rudolph are staying on at the hall for another

week,' he explained, 'so while Mama has company I decided I could take a few days off. You wanted to learn to ski — how many lessons have you had?'

'Not many — but Robert, I don't know how to thank you for the skis. They're such posh ones.'

'You will thank me best by learning to ski well. Up in the mountains we can ski every day. Does that please you?'

'It sounds lovely,' she said, 'but I don't much like the chair lifts.'

Robert laughed in his familiar, ebullient way. 'We shall drive up to the cabin and take the smaller slopes from there. An area set aside for beginners. When you are more confident we can go up higher in the chair lift and ski down.'

They had reached the farmhouse, where Robert had called earlier, so that her aunt and all the family knew of the proposed skiing trip.

'You can't go home to England without learning to ski properly,' her aunt said. Angela tried to hide the heartaches that this reminder prompted. At least she would enjoy this time with Robert; she would make the most of it and only at the last minute would she tell him she planned to go home earlier. If she did! Now, seeing Robert again she was less sure than ever of what to do.

'Ten o'clock, Angela,' said Robert as he left. 'No oversleeping, and you have plenty of time to wash your hair!'

Angela sensed an air of mystery in the living room when she returned. Grandma seemed to be hiding a smile, the men gave Angela a funny look before going back to the pigs, while Aunt Hilde was suddenly extremely busy in the kitchen.

Angela carried the glasses to the kitchen and started to wash up.

'Leave that, Angela,' her aunt said firmly. 'You must go to pack. Remember you'll need extra warm clothes, and a pretty dress for the evenings. There's a good hotel up there, and being New Year everyone will dress up.'

Angela sat in her room just staring into space. She was going up into the mountains with Robert, to a cabin. It sounded so romantic, yet beneath all the excitement lurked a fear that something dreadful would go wrong. An avalanche perhaps? Or was she going to break a leg?

Next morning she heard Robert arrive early, and watched him through the window talking to Josef. Again she felt a curious streak of fear run down her spine. Erika had said that he used women for revenge. What motive could he have for taking her on holiday with him? But when he came into the house, clean-shaven, fresh-faced and with a broad smile on his face, love overcame her apprehension.

He put her suitcase and skis in the back of the vehicle, which was already well loaded and, promising her aunt that he would take good care of her, they set off.

Through the snow-covered countryside they climbed higher and higher, the twisty road passing through villages and woods until it levelled out to a kind of plateau. They passed a large hotel, a typical Austrian house with carved wooden balconies, which in summer would be colourful with geraniums and petunias. Now the windows were shuttered against the cold. Beyond the hotel Robert drove along a narrow track among isolated smaller wooden houses and stopped at a long low building built in the shelter of a belt of trees.

Robert looked across at her and grinned. 'My winter residence,' he said, 'summer too when I have time.'

Already people were skiing.

'We have a small school here for beginners,' Robert explained as the instructor's voice came echoing across the valley, 'but at this time of year it is booked up well in advance. So, *meine liebling*, you will have to make do with me.'

'As long as you remember that I'm new to all this, and a bit scared,' she admitted.

'Not for long, Angela.' His smile was comforting, and so was the interior of the single-storey cabin. A wood stove in the centre of the room burned fiercely, so that the sudden change of temperature made her body tingle.

Thick rugs covered the floor, and there was a single bed or cot, with deep wooden sides, in each of the opposite corners.

Robert noticed her scrutiny. 'What could be more romantic than the two of us sharing a room? This isn't Vienna I'm afraid, Angela,' he said quietly. 'But I promise you that skiing is an energetic sport and we shall both need our sleep.'

She didn't answer — what was there to say? That she'd willingly take advantage of such a golden opportunity? But just to be his companion was enough. How long was it to be — one day? two? three? However long, it was a bonus she hadn't counted on, and in these surroundings she felt as if she had left her real self, with all her uncertainties, behind her. Here she was Robert's. For this brief magic spell he belonged to her.

'We do boast a kitchen and bathroom,' Robert was saying, opening doors. Angela wondered if she were expected to cook over the wood stove, but there was a small electric cooker too.

'Electricity up here?' she said.

'Yes, convenient for the village, but not so romantic. I have an arrangement with the hotel for one of the women to come in and clean and light the fire when I'm coming up here. But now, Angela, you can make the coffee.'

At last, a kitchen of her own! Robert had proved to be quite domesticated at the hall when allowed to be, but here she intended to do everything for her Hercules. While she prepared the coffee, he was opening boxes of provisions and stacking them away. Eva had prepared a quantity of food besides supplying packets of tinned food.

'Eva means us to stay for the rest of the winter,' Robert said, filling up the small fridge with bacon, eggs, sausages, milk and cream.

After drinking their coffee, they dressed up in ski-suits, bobble hats, mittens and dark glasses and walked to the beginners' slope by the pine wood.

Robert was pleased that Angela had learned at least the rudiments. What she lacked most was confidence, but Robert proved an unexpectedly patient tutor, and when they trudged back to the cabin an hour later she felt pleased with her progress.

'Mountain air makes you hungry,' Robert said, 'so we'll go over to the hotel for a meal.'

'I'd better shower and change then. What do I wear?'

'Something warm but pretty,' he said, and she selected a wool dress she knew he admired.

She had brought her dressing gown and, after a shower, returned wearing it. Robert had undressed and was wearing a bright orange towelling robe trimmed with black. He made a startling but attractive picture; the brightness of the colours suited his dark, well-weathered skin. When he came back from the shower Angela disappeared into the kitchen while he dressed.

'Angela.' His voice sounded suddenly behind her and she turned to find him standing at the doorway. 'I am not going to apologise for the lack of privacy here. We could go out of our way to make arrangements like hiding behind the kitchen door while the other changes, but I cannot stand hypocrisy. You don't have to look at me if you find me unattractive, but I like women to behave naturally.'

'You must make allowances for my English reserve,' she said. 'Besides, I don't know what my aunt and uncle would think — or your mother?' she reminded him with a mischievous twinkle in her green eyes.

'You have answered your own questions, Angela.' He

was, she noticed, pulling on some dark brown trousers over a pair of brown-patterned briefs. 'We don't have your English reserve. My mother and your relatives would not be the slightest bit concerned. And another thing, *liebchen*, you are only half English.'

'That's no excuse,' she said.

'So who needs excuses?' he flung over one tawny, powerful shoulder, as he went to put on a brown silk cravat and cream-coloured shirt. With a dark brown velour sweater on top, Angela thought how magnificent he looked.

She went to the mirror on the wall between the two beds to comb her hair. Robert's face appeared in the reflection above hers.

His dark hair was thick and strong, but set in vigorous waves on his strong, squarish head.

Angela moved away. 'Now I suppose we shall quarrel or something,' she said.

'Why should we do that?' he asked, looking puzzled.

'Looking in the same mirror together. Oh, I don't know, some silly superstition my English grandmother used to repeat.'

'What shall we quarrel about?' Robert asked with amusement.

'We won't,' she said adamantly, then in a softer voice she added, 'we mustn't spoil anything, it's so lovely here.'

Robert turned away from the mirror to face her. 'And I thought you would complain of the cold,' he said brightly.

Angela laughed as she put on her sheepskin coat and high-legged boots. You don't notice the cold when you're so hopelessly in love, her heart whispered.

He kept her hand in his as they walked along the icy track to the hotel. The dining room reminded her of Robert's baronial hall, with shields, swords and antlers on display, and the dark wooden tables and chairs with their red checkered tablecloths looked inviting.

There was still an air of Christmas festivity about the place and as they sat close together in an intimate dining cubicle Angela believed she had never felt so contented in the whole of her life. But her contentment was short lived.

As more people began to assemble for dinner, Angela recognised some of Robert's colleagues from the conference in Vienna, and after dinner Robert escorted her back to the cabin explaining that they were going to hold a short business meeting at the hotel.

She sat for a while by the stove trying to read, but her thoughts kept straying. Robert hadn't come here simply to enjoy her company. Teaching her to ski was just a way of passing the time before more important affairs in the evening. She felt resentment that she had been used. She wondered if Erika was here.

In low spirits she undressed and got into bed. Voices from the hotel were wafted back towards the trees and occasionally, when a door opened somewhere, she could hear the distant strains of music.

Angela switched off the light but the cabin was illuminated by soft flickering flames from the stove. She snuggled deeper beneath the feather-filled quilt, just peeping out to watch the shadows which made pictures on the walls . . .

* * *

'I am waiting for my English breakfast,' a loud voice demanded across the cabin.

Angela couldn't seem to wake up. She was warm and deliciously comfortable. A finger tickled her ear, and she tried vainly to shake it off. Robert ran his fingers through her hair and dropped a tantalising kiss in the curve of her neck as his hand crept underneath the quilt.

She opened her eyes to see a pair of long legs in striped pyjamas standing by her bed. He whisked away the quilt to reveal Angela respectably covered in brushed cotton pyjamas, and bent to nuzzle her neck. For a few minutes she revelled in his horse-play, then remembered that he hadn't been in when she had dropped off to sleep.

'What time is it?' she asked sleepily.

'Time you were cooking my breakfast!' He lifted her bodily out of the cot and carried her over to the fire.

'What is this?' he questioned in mock reproach. 'Do you think pyjamas will help to keep me under control?' He laughed sarcastically. 'I told you I love women, and I expect them to be feminine. You are not a student now, Angela.' He fetched her dressing gown from the wardrobe. 'Wear this!' he said.

She snatched the gown and disappeared into the bathroom.

Surveying herself in the long bathroom mirror, she stepped into her dressing gown and zipped it up. Mm . . . it *was* a bit clingy, more so than she had realised. No wonder Robert preferred it to the shapeless pyjamas.

When she got to the kitchen he was making coffee and had already placed several rashers in a heavy frying pan.

'Like to do it over the wood stove?' he asked. 'Primitive — but then we are primitive, aren't we?'

'Speak for yourself,' she retorted. 'I've never cooked over a stove like that, but if that is how your lordship . . .'

She picked up the pan, and soon the cabin smelt of sizzling bacon, making her feel very hungry. Robert came to watch, which made her feel certain she'd break one of the eggs, so she cracked them into a cup and slid them neatly into the pan to avoid nervous accidents.

Robert ate heartily. 'That was very good, Angela. If you weren't going home I would suggest that we retire Eva from the kitchen.'

Did he know about her letter from Christopher and that wretched air ticket? Had Josef or Aunt Hilde told him?

'I don't think your mother would approve of that idea,'

Angela said, eating her own breakfast with more moderate enthusiasm.

He looked up from his plate and caught her admiring him — for his bathrobe had opened. Angela hastily looked away, her cheeks turning pink, but not before she had experienced that divine glow of affinity which she could only liken to Rudolph and Lilli's relationship.

'I think my mother would approve, and Eva, too, perhaps, if it meant she could stay in bed these cold winter mornings.'

Angela was sure Robert didn't visualise those mornings as she herself was doing. In her dream, a wild fantasy, they were married and on cold winter mornings they would sit together and enjoy an English breakfast which she had cooked just as they were doing now.

She felt acutely aware of her nakedness beneath her gown, just as she was conscious of his body throbbing with virility. She wanted to get up, go behind him and run her hands all over his broad chest, and for him to reach up and unzip her gown.

'You're eating slowly this morning,' he reprimanded her. 'The mountain air should be making you ravenous.' He poured more coffee for both of them, and Angela wondered how long she could keep up her pretence of indifference...

Once out in the cold clear air she was obliged to concentrate on learning to ski. She was improving, Robert told her.

In the evening, when they dined again at the hotel restaurant, Angela was almost afraid to look round in case Erika was there. But she wasn't, although there were plenty of other women with whom Robert seemed friendly. They strolled back to the cabin together, and Angela prepared for bed by the light of the fire while Robert was in the bathroom. She was so tired that she fell asleep straight away.

During the next two or three days, as she worked hard to please Robert, she knew that the barrier between them was slowly crumbling, that her decision had been made . . .

Robert was so pleased with her efforts that he decided they should to up on the ski lift to a higher slope. Having reminded her again of how to stop, he set the pace with Angela following. It was invigorating to feel the wind whistling past her ears. She forgot her nervousness and felt proud of the way she followed in Robert's wake, but she also forgot caution, and when Robert shouted to her to stop her skis slipped away from her. Suddenly she was falling and sliding, while the sky seemed to be revolving round her.

She was stunned for a few seconds and came to with Robert's laughter echoing over the snow. He was standing looking down at her undignified posture. Her sticks were gone and her skis too. Her limbs felt numb and she glared furiously at Robert. How *could* he laugh at her? She might be seriously injured.

She was aware of a clump of trees to her right; she couldn't imagine how she'd got there. Robert was still laughing as he dropped on his knees between her spread-eagled legs.

'It's not funny,' she said hotly, gritting her teeth.

'You fell beautifully, *meine lieb*,' he said, and she felt his fingers at her ankles, moving upwards to her knees, her thighs and the gentle pressure at the pelvic region as he watched her expression.

'You haven't broken anything, I'm glad to say,' he assured her.

'How do you know? You don't know where I hurt,' she snapped. She wasn't really hurt at all, she was surprised to discover, but she had to blame someone for her mistake. 'You shouldn't have told me to stop!'

'I thought you were being a little too confident. It isn't

the first time you've fallen and it won't be the last.'

'Oh yes it will,' she said. 'I'm not going to ski any more.'

But the dizziness she felt was not caused by her fall so much as the nearness of Robert, and the warm, embracing look in his velvety brown eyes.

'You'll get up and ski now,' he told her, but he was unzipping her ski-suit running his hands over her slim body until she trembled. Several skiers plunged past them quite close, but Angela was hardly aware of them. She felt the warmth from Robert's hands flooding through her body. One of the skiers shouted some joke about causing an avalanche.

'We could, couldn't we, Angela? There is enough passion between us to cause an avalanche,' he said huskily, and she found herself wishing he would unzip his dark red ski-suit. Then he picked up a handful of snow and began packing it inside her ski suit. She fought and struggled, but he didn't let her up until he had zipped her up again with the snow melting inside.

'You rotten swine,' she said breathlessly, hitting out at him. 'It's all wet and sticky, and you've spoilt my new suit.'

He caught her aggressively against himself. 'But you aren't going to ski again,' he taunted. 'However, you do have to get down this slope to the cabin.'

'My sticks have gone, and my skis,' she moaned.

'No, they haven't, I have them. Now listen carefully and do as I say.'

'I can't do it, Robert. Couldn't we just walk?' she begged.

'You follow me down and stop complaining!'

She couldn't get back to the cabin quick enough to get out of the wet suit. Robert took an easy run down, walking through a pine wood and then skiing the last slope until they could see the hotel.

'There,' he said, 'that wasn't so bad, was it?'

She grinned sheepishly. 'At least I can say I went up in the chair lift and skiied down, even if I cheated and slid a few metres.'

'You need to do it every day for at least two weeks,' Robert said, and as they walked up the lane to the cabin, skis like rifles over their shoulders, a tremulous silence fell between them. Angela could see no chance of returning to this idyllic haven. Even if she stayed in Austria, she had the feeling that this might be Robert's last fling with his English secretary.

Robert unlocked the door. They propped the skis up against the cabin wall on the veranda and, inside, took off boots and ski suits.

'Yuk!' Angela exclaimed as icy particles fell out of hers. 'That was a mean thing to do,' she said without malice.

Robert took her suit and shook it well.

'It's only water. We'll hang it up. It will soon dry.'

Angela threw logs on the fire so that it crackled and hissed excitedly.

'Out of those wet clothes,' Robert ordered, and fetching her dressing gown he insisted that she strip completely.

She didn't argue. Out there on the mountain he had joked about the passion between them, but it wasn't a joke to Angela. He could flirt and tease, play his frivolous little tricks, and she took it all in good part, because she loved him. The thought of their eventual parting caused her intense pain.

Angela knelt on the fur rug by the stove, letting the warmth seep right through to her bones. Her cheeks were rosy and her green eyes glowed.

Robert brought her a cup of tea, then, after removing his sweater, he stood before the mirror shaving with an electric razor.

'You're getting ready early,' she said.

'As chairman I ought to go over to the hotel and check on arrangements for this evening. You can come too, but you might like the cabin to yourself to get ready without me pestering you.'

'What time shall I come over then?' she asked.

'I'll come back for you. By the way, I'd like you to wear that little pale blue dress with the fringe tonight.'

Angela got up and went over to the wardrobe, pulling out the blue dress.

'This one?' she asked, doubtingly. 'It's a bit bare for this weather . . . '

'It suits you. You'll look like an ice maiden,' he said, without turning away from the mirror.

It was New Year's Eve; everyone would be in party mood. But she didn't feel like going to a party. She would much rather have stayed in the warm cabin with Robert. Tomorrow they would be going down to the valley, and after that . . . ?

After Robert left the cabin, Angela sighed in despair. When she had first started to work for him he had suggested that his secretary should be his mistress too. Now when she was ready to play the game according to his rules, he had changed his mind.

She showered, taking her time, wishing that her hands were Robert's. She smiled, remembering the way he had felt her all over after her tumble, and then smothered her with snow.

Robert had brought out in her such a blaze of passion that Christopher ('never more than lukewarm') would never have believed it. She wrapped the big fluffy towel around her and went out to dry herself by the stove.

By the time Robert returned, she was ready.

'Let me look at you,' he said and she pivoted round for his approval.

'You never let me down, Angela,' he praised her. 'And as you know I expect a lot from my secretary.'

She smiled at him wistfully, glad that he had chosen this dress.

11

'Had I better wear my boots and carry my evening shoes?' she asked Robert when she couldn't stand his scrutiny any longer.

'We'll go in the car, but I'll carry you over the snow,' he said in a mellow tone.

She put on her skeepskin coat and carried her shawl. Snow was falling again, to her surprise. Confined in the cabin, the windows shuttered, once darkness fell, there was no way of telling that the weather had changed.

Robert locked the door, put the key in his coat pocket and swept her up in his arms. She was reluctant to go to the party, but perhaps after all it was best.

After dinner tonight there was to be dancing, Robert explained. To Angela it was just like an extension of the conference in Vienna, as all the same people were present. She was pleased to renew the acquaintance of some of those she had met previously, especially as Robert had to circulate a great deal. And of course, she realised, he had brought her here for the same reason he had taken her to Vienna: she was his secretary. At least she had lasted more than three months in the job.

They were in the middle of their meal when some late comers arrived. Robert immediately got to his feet and went to greet Erika, who was with the small middle-aged man Angela had seen in Vienna.

Angela felt her body stiffen with irritation. So behind all this, a clandestine meeting had been arranged. Who was the man — another scapegoat like herself? All very convenient: Robert would report back to his mother that Erika was with someone else?

Angela's bitterness grew until she couldn't bear it any longer. She got up and went towards the ladies' room. In the corridor outside the men's coats hung on pegs along the wall. She found Robert's and in a second she was holding the key to the cabin. Retrieving her own coat, she slipped it on and hurried to the main doors. Her thin-soled shoes were little protection against the snow, but she struggled on against an icy wind until she reached the cabin.

Thankful to get inside, she warmed up the percolator and knelt by the stove drinking coffee. Hatred built up inside her until she was in a frenzy of anger. No, no, no! She would not be a pretty little thing tagging along behind Robert so that people wouldn't notice his liaison with Erika.

In a blind fury she took off her clothes and put on her dressing gown. She got out her suitcase and began throwing her things into it, her mind tight with torment as she mentally abused the great Robert.

She didn't hear him enter, but she did hear a calm voice behind her saying, 'Angela, what are you doing?'

His voice and the calmness of it took her by surprise. She swung round guiltily.

'Packing my things to go home,' she screamed at him. 'You only brought me along to pacify your mother — so that she won't have to imagine that it's Erika who's been sharing this cabin. Well, I'm not going to be your puppet any more!' Tears of anguish spilled over, and she screeched croakily. 'You said you expect your secretary to be your mistress but it's still Erika isn't it, and I suppose I'm too young and inexperienced to make you happy in bed? She was in Vienna too, wasn't she? You don't go anywhere without meeting her. Well, I did last longer than three months, and I've never been homesick, but . . . I'm going home to marry Christopher!'

As she finished with what was meant to be a cry of triumph over him, her voice failed her. Words tumbled out uncontrollably between the sobs. 'Only I don't love him, I'll never love him, because I love you, but you love Erika!'

Robert was shaking her hard.

'Stop this nonsense at once, Angela,' he said. She went limp and clung to him.

'Angela, *liebling*, what are you doing to me? To yourself? My darling, I love you — I love *you* — do you hear me?'

'Oh, Robert,' she moaned, reaching up to cling to his neck. She felt so ashamed of her outburst, of allowing Robert to see her cry, and then she realised what he had said.

'B-but you can't love me,' she sobbed. 'You love Erika.'

'No, Angela. I do *not* love Erika, nor have I ever loved her. I have only been trying to help her over a difficult period.'

'Then Lotte?' Angela cried in disbelief, 'Or this English girl?'

'The only English girl I ever loved — do love,' he whispered softly in her ear, 'is you, my precious.' He lifted her tear-stained face, and his mouth met her lips, gently at first, until he was hungrily manipulating her tongue to placate his.

Angela couldn't believe what was happening to her. She seemed to have lost all her strength and would have collapsed to the floor, but Robert held her tightly, kissing her as she relaxed in his arms.

'There was a girl in London,' he explained, 'but we were both very young. She came from New Zealand. I couldn't go there and she wouldn't come to Austria. But that was fifteen years ago! Lotte has been a friend of my family ever since I can remember.'

'And Erika?'

'Erika came to work for me. She fell in love with me, and

my mother made her leave. She threatened to take her own life, she was obsessed, infatuated — but that too is many years ago. Then she met Helmut and married him, as she thought, to spite me. She soon left him. I asked her to come to my party because I hoped to persuade her to go back to Helmut. Perhaps I also wanted her to see my pretty secretary . . . '

'So you did use me!'

'I fell in love with you the first time I met you. Why else would I invite you to be my secretary and expect you to live in my house?'

'To put Erika off,' Angela said with disappointment.

Robert sighed. 'Erika, Erika, Erika, always Erika. You are like my mother . . . I love you, Angela, but I cannot neglect my obligations. I feel a little responsible for Erika's unhappiness. I arranged for her to meet Helmut in Vienna. Now as you saw tonight, they are together again, and I hope they will stay together.'

He kissed her long and passionately. Then he sighed again. 'There is only one problem,' he said, 'I shall have to find another secretary.'

'Oh no you won't,' Angela said defiantly. 'I shall be your wife *and* your secretary for ever, Robert darling. No other woman is going to get near enough to fall in love with you.'

'And my lover too?' he whispered. 'Everyone assured me that you loved me, but I hardly dared to hope. I felt sure you must be homesick.'

'Never,' she answered decisively. 'Only lovesick. I told you, when I love someone I am at least faithful, no matter what.'

'Christopher? Andreas?' he reminded her.

'Mean nothing to me. What shall I do with that air ticket?'

'Tear it up — we'll get married at once, then we'll go to England in the spring, for your father's wedding. But first we're going to shut ourselves away in Paradise. We'll wave the others off tomorrow morning and have a honeymoon before the wedding.'

Robert laid her down on the rug, tenderly caressing all that he intended to possess before the night was through. He slid down the zip, pushed her gown over her shoulders as she stretched up to hold him close. She urged her soft white breasts against his hard chest and his fingers lightly explored the curves of her body as she arched towards him.

'I came to take you back to the party,' he whispered against her ear as passion blazed exhilaratingly between them.

She shook her head.

'Then we'll have to say you had a headache,' he said, and his body relaxed against hers, deliberately delaying his pleasure, cherishing her youthful beauty as she explored her Herculean baron.

'Oh, Robert,' she whispered. 'I've never loved like this before.'

'Nights were made for loving, *meine lieb*, and if you hear a distant rumbling you will know that we have started an avalanche!'